The Sixth Dimension Defined

Neil Vickers

The Sixth Dimension Defined

First paperback edition

Ethan Fosse Publications
Ethan.fosse10@gmail.com

978-1-80541-552-7 - paperback
978-1-80541-551-0 - eBook

Contents

CONTENTS

Chapter 1

———— ◆ ————

We gaze at the stars and wonder where they are, shining in an abyss of space, the stars in a dark place twinkling in another world far away. What happens in this strange place we know nothing about? At best, we can simply assume life exists beyond our imagination as we have only just arrived at our first two nearest planets, yet there are millions of stars in the sky – a sun for every galaxy; a light to guide the way into an undiscovered world where any form of being can exist in its own environment bringing life to a lost world.

Is there another dimension we can use to potentially discover what is virtually impossible in the physical world? Maybe we could teleport our minds into hyperspace and move from a fifth into a sixth dimension. Is it possible that our minds have transitioned, at lightning speed, through a supernova to other worlds to reach the ends of our imagination, only to emerge into a surreal world –a place where evolution has re-evaluated itself with endless time

– full of mystery and intrigue where you can only expect the unexpected?

We have to pay more attention to the human brain. No one has ever explored completely the human brain and its capability to take you into other dimensions that only exist in dreams; a fantasy world of mystical characters created from images where dreams are evolved in a sixth dimension and forms unknown to us. We only use a fraction of our capability. So, our vision is to take what we have and move it from a fifth to a sixth dimension where only the undiscovered live and thrive, on another level where oxygen to breathe is not necessary and food is not taken.

We are an all-American team working in micro-organisms discovering the ability to be able to reduce size in matter to a point where it's virtually invisible but still complete in its form. We had come so far in this field – we could reduce a rat to the size of an ant and it functioned as it did when it was normal size. We had come into a new dimension where we could now control matter. Yet, our main concern when shrinking the rodent was that it would no longer eat or drink and would die within a week.

We had to look at where we could go from here if they were not going to sustain life after shrinking. Why would we go on using a life form to experiment on? The team would have to get the formula right before we could progress to a human being. We could never be able to justify a human life in a macabre experiment...

Maybe we could try shrinking a human corpse to see whether it would reduce to a minimal size. We would need a body, and, if the shrinking was successful, somebody to be a volunteer to be shrunk in the same formatting as the corpse to demonstrate we could be successful with a live human and that the results were similar to the experiment with the rodent. At least the subject would be able to tell the team why they did not want to eat or drink when reduced in size and whether they, as a top predator, felt vulnerable with the fact they were now so small they had become food for mice and any other creature that could eat them.

They needed to move to the next stage where they would be virtually invisible to any predator that would look for them as food. We would have to have measures in place to be able to fight off any rodent or animal that could devour us in a moment – like an anteater, unknowingly to the termites, breaking into a termite mound and devouring the whole nest. We could not enter another stage and be vulnerable. After all, humans had become the top of the food chain and we would revert back to being prey for any hungry animals or organisms to come along. We needed to do more research on shrinking beyond visibility and to be able to protect ourselves from any harmful entities. We would not be sure what can of worms we would be opening and whether we could take the program forward knowing that it could end in catastrophic disaster.

We would have to look at how we would communicate in such a world where we were virtually invisible to all, maybe in a sixth dimension where matter no longer exists and time itself would be hard to measure. Would we still be able to live on this planet or could we transport ourselves to another galaxy where beings had evolved above us to another form not known or thought about by us? It would be an epic journey into the unknown. The universe was endless as we knew it, so there would be no boundaries in space travel. It was going to be a bit different than a day at the seaside. This was not going to be for the faint-hearted; it was going to be an incredible journey filled with mystery and suspense. It was going to be a complete life-changer; it was incomprehensible. What was going to take place to enable us to look into the future? We were going to go where we had only ever dreamed about, using space travel and all it encompassed.

Chapter 2

———— ◆ ————

We were nearly there as explorers – probably the greatest explorers the world has ever known. We would be pioneers and ambassadors for the earth; only the five of us would know we were going to discover new worlds never before seen by man. We would be the first to encounter strange planets supporting life, although we cannot comprehend any form of life beyond being human in any form. We would have to accept everything would be so different to what we know – beings that are nothing like us, that are primitive to us or have developed beyond our mindset, living in a surreal environment where only they can survive.

We would be able to be there to see the births of new planets as old ones die off, become unstable and break up into pieces to form new meteorites, like in the Orion belt, which will travel in space until they reach the suns in other galaxies and burn up in the heat of their rays. This could be the most inspiring voyage ever, unparalleled in any other way. At this stage of our journey, we could only imagine what would be out there waiting for us on our mission of discovery.

We were ready for the unknown; we just had to confirm our calculations before we took what could be an irreversible step into new worlds and galaxies, unknown and beyond us, in the darkness of space. Our brains would teleport us at a speed nobody could comprehend or understand. We had taken the human mind to a place never encountered. We would be evolving into mind-blowing intergalactic travellers.

We needed to see what was out there waiting to be discovered. As humans, we had been given an intelligence portfolio that had never been accessed and the power of thought was incomprehensible in its entirety. We were unsurpassed in our field in the psychic telepathy of the human brain and its ability to go beyond what we believed, projecting us at hyperspeed into a sixth dimension. There, words would have to be rewritten, calculations revised, new terminology invented for communication, languages decoded, signals formatted… the list was endless as there was no reckoning all the captivating beings we would encounter on our mission.

Where speed was in billiseconds, no other source of matter would ever travel at this speed never mind measure it. Coming close to it had only been a dream we could never ever realise. Trilliseconds would soon be the norm and billiseconds would be a measure of the past. You would never feel yourself travelling – you would have reached a destination before you thought about it. No more sick bags on the aeroplane – there would be no air sickness as you would not know travel as a way of moving.

We would move into the sixth dimension and be an energy source; nothing more. There would be no start or final destination, just one point of arrival or no return.

We would have to make sure we could get back to our bodies. We had no comprehension of how long our energy source would last, so our dread would be us being lost in space in some faraway galaxy, drifting forever in a darker place with no hope of return. We would be remembered as pioneers of space, the true explorers of all the galaxies, embroiled in what we did best… space travel for the future generations of our earth.

We would have set milestones of space travel and laid down paths of information for future travellers to encounter in their explorations into other worlds never before seen or conquered by man. This would rewrite the history books for the foreseeable future and beyond. It would clearly define the boundaries that humankind could travel to, discovering the reality of undiscovered worlds and their previously unknown life forms. It would be a perilous journey, fraught with mystery and danger on an unimaginable scale. We could be taking microorganisms to foreign planets or bringing them back to Earth with disastrous consequences – they could destroy our world or us theirs.

Chapter 3

———◆———

W e would have to set a precedent for what precautions would be necessary and execute them, any damage limitations being confined to Earth. We would have to think of so many scenarios that would safeguard our environment without sacrificing the many for the few. We had hardly discovered what lies at the bottom of our oceans and yet we were going to be travelling possibly billions of miles into the unknown of space, beyond the stars we see every night in our sky… beyond our solar system into galaxies far in excess of what the human mind could understand. We would be the size of an atom in a universe of diversity, travelling so fast we would be invisible to the naked eye, even too fast for the best universal telescopes. Nothing would be able to track our speed or see our power source as it went by a million times faster than lightning.

We would have to synchronise ourselves to the same speed, longitude and latitude. We would be bending our minds beyond all comprehension and we believed we would be entering a new dimension unbeknown to anybody on Planet Earth. We had to make sure we had a way back from this epic journey we were about to undertake – maybe some kind of tracker beacon – it was merely a step into another world to evaluate where humans could live once we had destroyed our own world as we know it.

We called it Mother Earth but never respected the life it gave us all and how we had evolved into what we are now. We had come such a long way in such a short space of time. There would be no going back to normal space travel after our encounter with the unknown; the sixth-dimension world was not ours. We would be entering into what could be the creator's world of mystique and wonder. We might even be able to meet the creator and he may possibly show us his world. It might not be as we imagine – even the creator could have had his sleepless nights whilst forming the endless boundaries in space.

Were we going to be overstepping the mark? We had all been instrumental in the obliteration of the human race over the years, destroying our planet to the detriment of human existence. So what if he should not approve of our unwanted intrusion into the privacy of his own space?

We would all have to hope that we could explore new worlds and benefit other planets with our presence, both in our galaxy and in others beyond. Taking such a leap into the unknown, bringing our inventions, medicines and knowledge to less advanced species, we could only guess that us reaching their planets in faraway solar galaxies would be beneficial both to humans on Earth and beings on undiscovered planets.

However, it could be a dangerous mission, with endless boundaries and fraught with peril; there were possible encounters with barbaric species beyond our own comprehension. We needed to finish off the fine-tuning ready for travel, as it would not be a walk in the park.

All the team would have to agree on a completion day to travel.

We could not give any clues as to what we were planning to do as the program could have been deemed too dangerous to proceed with and we could have been relegated back to jobs we were doing before our promotions into research. We had all been promoted together to work as a team but we had gone beyond our mandate of discovery of other planets to the exploration of them and the galaxy.

Adam and Blaise were working on travelling whilst Anthony, Savarnee and Amanda were focused on the shrinking and monitoring the progress of getting us ready to be shrunk. Would we be able to return to our normal size after shrinking? One would never really know, so it was suggested that the rats that had died could be brought back to normal size. Obviously, they would not be alive but at least we would know we could bring matter back to its original size. We then had to work on live rats to see if we could shrink and recover them back to normal size, alive, without loss of any brain or bodily functions.

We could only hope that our technology was advanced enough to be able to reverse the transformation and return things as they had been before.

Amanda was foremost in this field as her research into it was impeccable and flawless in practice. However, like everything we do, it was subject to abnormalities occurring in scientific technology – there were always going to be mistakes and fatalities. They were inevitable. It was also inevitable that there would be ongoing research into why, when and how the above happened. We had been told categorically that we could not do any research that could risk life – human or otherwise - and that we were merely a research facility, not here to increase the limits of our knowledge into the realms of eventual space travel.

Travelling through the galaxy would broaden our horizons to future colonization of other planets as our planet was moving towards becoming a toxic environment and we would soon have exhausted all oxygen-supporting plants and oxygen emissions from trees that support life.

Eventually, we would all be accepting that the planet was no longer fit to sustain human life. We had evolved over millions of years and yet virtually destroyed the Earth in less than 200 years.

We had to work on both jobs – what we were here for and getting paid to do, and also, all the other experiments and secret investigations, which would have to be kept top secret between the five of us.

We did not need to be inviting strangers into our new concept of life beyond earth; over-excitement would breed discontent in other scientists elsewhere who were keen to be part of the program. Only the five would be acceptable to progress with the transformation and the travel through space. Each of us needed to know all the risks and accept the conditions we were going into and the dangers we may encounter in our transformation and travels. The whole team was now geared up to take it to the next level.

Chapter 4

————◆————

Adam, who was a professor in microbiology, had spent years in research of human endeavours to install microchips into the brain to enhance the ability to go beyond the normal IQ and increase the power to the next level by creating a microchip that could stimulate the brain into another dimension and thinking on a level unknown to man. This took more of the form of an encrypted message being formatted into a computerised synchronised language that would only exist in the brain.

Anthony was Adam's assistant and was also a professor and a good friend of his. They had known each other since starting college together and had grown to appreciate each other and their abilities. Adam was a leader, and, although Anthony shared his knowledge, he fell behind Adam in his quest to move forward with his future experiments into colonial exploration. Supporting Adam's endeavours fell more into Anthony's comfort zone.

Blaise was an entity on his own – he was the man on computer programming. He could program the future of travel and co-ordinate the destinations and times of travel along with distance, speed, longitude and latitude. He would be instrumental in the movement through space; our planner and directional guide to get us there and back.

Savarnee's specialist field was in robotics. He had PhDs in robotic engineering and was the person most advanced in his field in America and possibly the world. He had brought robotics so far that they were nearly able to think like humans; it was becoming second nature to use them in warfare and security. They could now outrun and outshoot a man, and could even think like one. Blaise was instrumental in programming the computers within the robots and he was respected as the foremost designer in his field.

Amanda was an astrologist. She had a PhD in astrology, and she was also recognised as the best. She had written books on the expansion of the universe and was instrumental in mapping the galaxy and all of its asteroids that were on a trajectory to collide with Earth. She had been in charge of the space program at NASA looking into the challenges of a mission to Mars and working out the route of space travel and the trajectory around Mars for a possible space landing.

They all had knowledge of space travel, robotics and microorganisms, so the plan would have to progress to travelling. We needed to move our secret program forward to be able to travel. We had done the work on the rodents and that had been successful; however, the fact they died had left a big hole to fill. Now, we needed to experiment with a human body to see if it would come back perfectly; after all, we had all taken an oath to move everything forward.

We agreed we would meet at work in the morning to do the experiment, so we said goodnight and wished everybody well.

The morning came around fast; everyone in the group was excited. We had our human body to experiment with – it was a female of around 40 years old, a single lady with no family, who had died suddenly. The mortician had not had the body registered – he was a friend of Savarnee's and he had promised the body would be returned as soon as we had concluded the experiment.

We had to evaluate the body so the experiment would follow the same pattern as when we would be ready to shrink ourselves. Adam was ready on the trigger with the laser shrinker – he looked sweaty but excited as he would be the one shrinking the body. We had no idea what was going or coming back, so we all got our uniforms on and prepared to wear face protection whilst the laser would be in operation. It would take up to 10 bursts of the laser to shrink the body to a virtually invisible size, then we would have to examine the body to see what condition it was in. We had to discover whether it was in true form or if it had been mutated into some other form where only so much of it was recognisable. Although the rat had survived the transformation, the fact it would or could not eat was a disaster for the program; shrinking the corpse had to work.

We were ready for the countdown. Adam counted down:

"5, 4, 3, 2, 1 – lasering now!"

He hit the body with a flash of light, pumping 8 lasers into it. It was shrinking at a phenomenal speed – it was nearly down to the size of a rat and was still shrinking. Adam gave it two more on the laser; it had virtually disappeared. It was so amazing to see it shrink to virtually nothing in 10 jets of the laser. We would now need to examine the body to see how it looked. Adam was the first to have a proper look.

"Look, look!" he said. "It's really small but perfect."

As we all looked around it, we could see no imperfections in the body; it seemed it had all gone really well.

Chapter 5

——— ◆ ———

We needed to reverse the shrinking using a reverse laser that would put the energy and matter back into the body and make it standard size again. Adam hit it again and the body started to grow but it was struggling to recover from the shrinking. We could only get it back to half its original size. We would have to think about it before we hit the laser again; it could lead to further problems. We had to get it right before we could move into space travel; it seemed we would need a lot more research. Only time would tell if we would be able to travel at all.

It seemed the experiment had gone wrong, and coming back as a smaller body would not be a good thing. We needed to be able to return to our original forms and that was all there was to it.

Our day had been a day of deliberation and exploration into the unknown; nothing had ever been practiced before. We were well on the way to making history in being able to shrink matter and it returning back to its form as before. Only the final stage remained. We would discuss the body in the morning so we all said goodnight and started on the trip home.

Amanda lived near Adam.

"Can I have a lift?" she asked.

"No," Adam replied.

Amanda asked, "Why not?"

Adam was just being his normal self and said, "Come on then," and Amanda got into the car.

On the way home, they discussed how disappointed they were with the outcome and how the body never came back to full size.

"Could it be that you did not give it enough laser to bring it back to full size?" Amanda suggested.

"No!" Adam replied. "I can't understand why the body did not come back to full size; it will be on my mind all night. I'm looking for a reason why – it is the law of physics that what you put in you should get out. I don't understand what went wrong. It can only be that I need to up the power source so it will increase the laser going into the body. I'm not sure overdoing the times lasered would work; it would more than likely just fry the body."

"We will have to have a look in the morning. I'm feeling sad about the body. The person it belonged to will have to be buried half the size!" Amanda started laughing uncontrollably. "The poor woman…" she said, laughing until she was crying, "…only half a body. It's your fault, Adam – she will meet you one day and pay you back."

Adam laughed and said, "She will have to find me first." We got into our area and Amanda was still smiling from ear to ear. Still managing a small giggle, Adam said, "It isn't funny."

"I'm sorry but it is to me," replied Amanda.

Adam went to bed that night with a heavy heart, just wondering if he could have done more to keep everything normal. He had arranged to pick up Amanda in the morning, and fortunately, the night went so fast.

During the morning car ride, Adam said to Amanda, "I thought I would be up most of the night thinking but I must have been really tired. I was trying to backtrack to see if I had not exactly repeated the procedure in the same way as when we shrunk the body."

Amanda said, "Don't worry; if she comes back alive, you will have to grow longer arms to take your new girl-friend out."

Adam laughed. "You're funny, you are. It's ok for you saying that – it was not your responsibility."

"One thing about it," Amanda said, "at least they can save money on the coffin size."

Amanda was laughing out loud.

"Very funny, Amanda," Adam said. "It's not really funny at all. I will get my own back on you when you direct us in space somewhere and you end up in a different galaxy on your own; you won't be laughing then."

"Don't get too touchy, Adam. I was only joking." "Well, yes, but a joke is a joke; now let's leave it."

Amanda thought, 'Well, that's telling me then. I best keep quiet or I will be walking to work and that would make Adam happy.'

We arrived and met the rest of the team in reception for a coffee. We had to be quiet and not talk about our experiment, only the work we were doing for the company. We all collated information that was going to be needed for the company. Only Savarnee had the keys to our science laboratory because of the secret work we did for the company.

The cleaners were only allowed in for one hour whilst we were watching their movements and making sure they were not stealing any information. That would be classed as espionage. It was good for our own experiments that it was so secure and even management needed a pass to go through security. It was a walk in the park for us as we were only a small team, known well by the security staff, so it allowed us to be discrete in what we did.

That made us all special; we were the best at what we had achieved in our work and the government recognised it and was instrumental in the freedom within the sphere that we were researching and they would support our findings in what we called our monthly service accounts.

They obviously knew nothing about our other research into universal travel. This would only be released to the government when we had completed our mission into the unknown.

Anthony said, "Let's go and see how our body is faring. It is likely to be decomposing as we have no proper refrigerated storage and she is standing up in our fridge with the shelves out. I hope the cleaners didn't go in the fridge. That would give them a real fright." We would have to tell them there was no cleaning needed in the laboratory today as it was sufficient for purpose and experiments would be taking place.

We all got into the laboratory and the body was out of the fridge, on the floor, at full size! It had outgrown the fridge and fallen out into the laboratory. It was a good job we had arrived early before the cleaners.

Anthony looked up and said, "Adam deserves some credit for his work," and they all thanked Adam. He had completed his work well; the problem was a delayed reaction to the laser which could have been down to the person being deceased. We were all happy it was back to normal and that meant we could now look at other avenues... like experimenting on a real human being.

Chapter 6

———◆———

Anthony was up for being the guinea pig but Adam said that this would not be good as we could not risk the program by losing one of the team. We would have to look elsewhere for a willing volunteer. If we lost one of the team, that could be disastrous for the research as everybody had their own part to play in the mission so there could be no risk to any member of the team.

We just had to find a person for the right reasons. Money was always a good deal-maker; it would always win through, so now all we had to do was match the right person to the money and everything would be ready to go. We would have to put everything on hold until we found the right person for the program. Amanda suggested Adam could be the person. Adam took the bait –

"Why me?!" he cried out.

Amanda started laughing again, so much she gave herself hiccups and had to have a glass of water to calm the hiccups down. She was on form, and where it was usually Adam making all the jokes, for the last day it had been Amanda's turn; Adam had not been expecting to hear it from her.

Blaise suggested he could put an advert on Facebook or other social media to get a quick response, but it would have to read right. Our problem was if we actually killed the person, we could all be arrested for manslaughter. It was a risk we might have to take, but a massive risk also to the life of the person acting as a guinea pig.

Savarnee said, "Well, we can make sure they know the risks and sign that they were taking part in an experiment and it could end in disaster."

Unfortunately, this applies only in wartime so we would have to answer for our research if it went wrong. We were all in it together; there would be no mercy shown at a court hearing. We all decided Blaise should go through with placing the advert, but it would have to be a lure with a reasonable fee. We had a slush fund available to us but it was ring-fenced to the discovery project we were working on.

Savarnee and Anthony had been chatting and Anthony said, "Well, I think if we can cover the pot of money from our personal accounts, if all goes well, we can just borrow the money from our work's slush fund and put it back later." We all agreed it would be the way to go. It all had to be kept secret and we would have to blindfold the person answering the advert while leading them into the building; meanwhile, some of us would distract the guards.

We had worked out already how we were going to get the person into the building – Blaise would turn off the camera system remotely for a minute whilst we got the person into the laboratory – but first, we needed the person. Blaise had advertised and the advert read: 'Person required for research project; earn quick money. Apply stating project space'. We all agreed on the advert and it was online within an hour. So far, we had 11 applicants for the job. Anthony would be the interviewer and he could do it from the coffee shop around the corner from work.

Blaise had created a new e-mail purely for the advert, which would be deleted after the person had been chosen. It would have to be somebody young and fit enough to absorb the laser properly and for their organs to withstand the shrinking and enlarging within a short time. Once it could be proved it could work, we would have no more need for the subject to take place in any more experiments. The rest was classified and not for eyes and ears beyond our team.

Blaise had booked the applicants in at 10-minute intervals, which would be enough time for Anthony to ask the questions he needed to ask. The main question would be 'Are you fit enough to take part?' He was finding it difficult to tell them they were going to be shrunk to the size of an ant or less and then, when they were at the shrunken size, he would be asking them how they felt. Amanda and Adam both burst out laughing, Amanda uncontrollably.

"How would you feel if you came in for some money and they shrunk you to an ant's size and were asking how you feel?" Anthony had a quieter laugh but his body was shaking inside trying to suppress his own laughter. It was just going to be a strange request when you're spider bait and they were asking how you feel.

Anthony spoke up – "I think if you told them what you were doing, they would not sign up for it. We would have to check for spiders as we don't know where in the room they could end up when shrinking took place. It could be near a skirting board around the floor area and a spider could run out and capture a morsel of food.

It would be too late to get the person back from behind the skirting board, we would have lost our person, and how would we be able to explain that the subject was shrunk and a spider ran off with them for a snack?"

Anthony was really concerned whilst all the rest of the team were smiling, almost at the point of bursting out laughing again.

Anthony said, "It's not funny! We have a heavy responsibility to ensure the safety of the subject and you're not taking it seriously."

As he said 'seriously', everybody burst out laughing again, even Anthony.

We all managed to stop laughing and Anthony said, "But seriously, we have to be professional in our approach to all this as there is going to be a long way to go to reach our goals."

Blaise had pencilled all the appointments in for the morning, so Anthony would stay away from the lab and come in late morning after the interviews. We all agreed to be more professional at work and respect the subject when he or she arrived.

Amanda said, "How are we going to tell them when they arrive that they're going to be shrunk?"

"You will need a potty for them to poo in!" said Adam.

Everybody laughed. I don't think anybody had thought about actually standing them in front of the laser, and the subject staying, still wondering what the hell was going to happen.

They would be running for the hills!

Maybe we could give them a coffee or tea drugged with a sleeping pill, but we really wanted to know what was happening to them as they were shrinking, whether they were in pain or relaxed as the laser started to work.

Amanda said it would be an astonishing thing to see them alive and shrinking.

Adam remarked, "Really? Are you sure? You sound a bit woozy in the head."

We appeared to have a real problem; we would have to be able to drug the subject even if it was a relaxer just to stop them moving as the laser started to shrink them.

Adam said, "You're more likely to need a diaper for the subject when they see me behind that machine. I'm not sure if I have it in me to laser a living person. I feel I will have been the one that's killed them if it all goes wrong. We haven't got enough evidence to prove, one way or another, whether the subject will live or die. Could we all justify the possible loss of a human life in pursuit of the future of travel? Is it that important I meet new species and go where people have never been before?"

"Yes," Amanda said. "It's one life that can save the world for future travel, to colonise different planets and to be pioneers of space. What could be better than one human life lost so that no one else has to die in our pursuit of space travel."

"I'm not sure I will let Anthony do his interviews," Adam said. "I'm not sure what we can tell them in an induction as to what they are going to be doing in their job description. We may as well say from the outset they're going to be a guinea pig in a macabre experiment that means, if it goes wrong, you could live the rest of your life the size of an ant, or worse still, die."

Blaise said, "Well, I can't see anybody accepting that as the advert I put in is slightly misleading. Lol, it doesn't say anything about the outcome of the experiment and that you could come back dead."

Adam said, "Come on, Blaise, you know it's a dangerous game we play. This is ground-breaking research; there are always casualties of war."

"I wasn't aware we were at war," Blaise said.

"No?" Adam replied. "Well, why don't *you* apply for the position? We might have some peace if you were shrunk. No one would be able to hear you."

"That's not nice," Blaise replied.

"Well, if the cap fits…" Adam said.

Amanda said, "Stop arguing, you two, or I will laser you both!"

"Oh, that's good," Adam said. "What will you do when I'm not here? It will be anarchy in here without me holding the team together! Let's make a plan and see who turns up for the experiment."

Blaise had said he would sort out interviews for the next morning, but it seemed as if everything took days to organise. If only things moved faster, we would be further into the experiment, but we had work to do for the company or risk losing our jobs and that would be a catastrophe to the program.

Chapter 7

———— ♦ ————

One of our jobs was to measure in space the limits of the laser in terms of distance and altitude. We had adapted it to shrink people which was a far cry from our remit. We had created a weapon that could shrink armies coming to our shoreline – it was now more of a military hardware laser and we had converted it in an easy revision to its primary use. We were possibly looking at a custodial sentence if we were caught using it for other reasons, so hopefully, we would have the applicant in the morning. We would have to be professional in our approach to interviewing them and revealing the experiment we were going to engage in. Then, if it worked, it would be world-breaking news that we could never reveal.

Our destiny was in space travel and we were getting ready to teleport ourselves into faraway galaxies. Tomorrow was going to be our big day.

We would start the program immediately. We had to tell them it was a machine for cleaning bugs and viruses off the person to save alarming them into thinking it was for something else. We needed to ensure they were calm and relaxed before we zapped them into a morsel of the person they were before. Now, we would have to call it a day – we were all scheduled to come in early tomorrow as we had a long day. We would have to leave at least four hours before bringing the subject back to life-size.

We met the team in the morning. Blaise said there were 12 for interviews, the last being around 10.30 am.

Savarnee said, "Plenty of time for shrinking!"

Adam replied, "Don't use that word again. You will scare off our candidates."

"Let's grab a coffee," Amanda said, "and go direct to the laboratory. We can tell the guards we are showing potential scientists around the laboratory in a view to taking on a new member of staff."

The guards would not be able to comprehend what we were really doing in the laboratory. The first candidate had arrived – a 72-year-old man who was struggling to get through the door.

"Not a good candidate for the job," Amanda whispered to Savarnee.

"No," he said, "if we shrink him and ask him what's wrong with him, we would be here all day listening."

We had to have someone younger so that their organs would recover from the laser. We quickly conducted the interview and moved through the next five – they were all males of at least 70. Six down out of the twelve – most were retired or jobless, homeless people just needing a cashflow to help them out with day-to-day living.

Then, a young-looking lady came in.

"Sorry I'm slightly late," she exclaimed. "I can see you have a queue of people sitting outside."

"That's ok," Adam replied.

Savarnee had learned she had recently been made redundant and needed to keep a roof above her head. She was very attractive and well-presented. After the interview, Adam said, "Can I have a word, Savarnee?" We had a conversation about the lady – it seemed Adam did not want to experiment on such a beautiful woman. She was too pretty and classy to be a guinea pig for our experiment. Adam said there was no way, then we all agreed everybody was pretty in their own way and their lives were all worth exactly the same. Good looks and class did not make their lives any more or less precious than everybody else.

Adam said she had not lived her life at the moment and she had some living to do before putting her life at risk.

He went on, "We need someone that has led a reasonable life."

We all had a good feeling that the experiment would go without risk but we agreed we would have to wait for an older person to come in for interview.

Looking down the list, Amanda said, "We have two people in their mid-40s waiting; let's give them a try."

The woman came in first. She was around 45. She was a good candidate, slim, with a nice personality. She wanted the money for an operation for her son who was poorly. We said we would let her know if she was successful and asked if she could wait outside. In came a man, around the same age, slightly overweight and breathless – he was not suitable for the position. We had a sneaky look at the others waiting. They all seemed like homeless street people… very sad for them but not suitable for our program. We decided to take the previous lady, who was waiting outside, thanked the others and said the job vacancy had been filled.

Before we called the lady in, we decided to call her by her first name, Joy, and explain to her the experiment she would be taking part in. We could not lie as to what the outcome would be, so we called Joy in and explained the process. She said she would put her own life at risk for the sake of her son; he needed the operation to live and Joy wanted the money to pay for the operation. Amanda promised she would take the money to the hospital if anything happened during the experiment. Joy said she did not want them to explain what was going to happen – her thoughts were solely about the money to help her child to live the life he had not lived.

Joy said, "I need the money and risking my life is worth it if my son lives. Do whatever you want to do; my body is yours."

The whole team were nearly reduced to tears – that this lovely woman would give her own life to save her son… she was to be adored for her sacrifice. We were all hoping that would not be the case and that it would simply be a process and she would not die… we all had our fingers crossed.

"Will it hurt?" she asked.

Savarnee assured her it should not be painful and that she was more likely to be scared of the laser than hurt by it.

Joy said, "Well, can we get on with it now? The longer I wait the less chance my son has of living."

We all had a chat and decided we were good to go and we would just have to spend an hour making sure all the laser and recording equipment was working.

It had to work now for us. Joy had brought some decency into the program; it was not about the project anymore but the vulnerability of the people taking part in the experiment and their wellbeing and safety; not the end goal or prize. It was all about common decency and looking after the wellbeing of our fellow man – nothing was more important and Joy had shown that to us today. We were all grateful for the sacrifice she was about to make, so we all wished her well and she stood in front of the laser.

Adam went behind and made some adjustments to the distance and said, "Ok, we are ready to go."

The team acknowledged him and, in unison, said "Go." Adam's hands were sweating as he went to pull the trigger. There was a beautiful lady standing in front of him and this could be her last day alive on earth. She smiled as Adam pulled the trigger multiple times.

Chapter 8

---◆---

She was disappearing before their eyes; she showed no signs of distress as the laser evaporated her body to a minute size. Within twenty seconds, she was hardly visible. We looked down. She was so tiny, it was like the Statue of Liberty looking down over us. The size difference was staggering. Only Amanda approached her so as not to frighten her; after all, she would have had no idea what was going to happen. Joy was now slightly bigger than an ant. Amanda had a microphone and wore a hearing piece to be able to hear and communicate with Joy.

First of all, Amanda asked, "How do you feel, Joy?"

"Very small!" she shouted back.

We weren't sure whether Joy was saying it as a joke or if that was how she really felt. Amanda decided not to proceed with that line of questioning so she then asked how she felt in herself.

Joy said, "Just some of the same aches and pains in the same places." This told the team that these normal pains would always remain no matter how small you were. Amanda asked about her appetite.

Joy said, "Strangely enough, I feel hungry." That was music to the ears of the entire team as, in previous experiments with the rodents, they had not eaten, and yet a live human felt hungry.

We gave her the smallest piece of cake and she said it was the size of a large rock but was enjoying the meal with no ill effects. Could we have been successful in our mission to be able to take things to the next step? Our goal was to travel into space at the speed of light and beyond, into the outer limits; not the final frontier but the start of an adventure beyond the limitations of mankind.

It would be the pinnacle of an enduring adventure and the beginning of discovery into the unknown where unexpected would be the new norm and the next adventure would be to a world without limits where normal, as we know it, no longer exists. We had to make sure the sacrifice Joy was making was a special contribution to our efforts to conquer space, its galaxies and frontiers. Speed would be no longer measured in miles a trillisecond – speed now would be faster than light itself and measured in zenicoms that were more than 100 times faster than a trillisecond. In this new world, we could not measure the new speeds we would now be travelling at.

Four hours passed after the experiment and Joy seemed to be coping well. She had more of an appetite than less and she had eaten a lot of the cake crumb. We had given her a saucer of water to drink out of, but to her, it had been the same size as a small lake. It was big enough to swim in! She appeared to be ok, but the proof of our hard work would be known when she was brought back to her original size and whether she would be able to walk and talk as she did before. Would she be back to some kind of normality? We could only hope she would come back to her original form but the human body and brain are so complex that one digit short could be disastrous to her wellbeing and transformation back into a normal size and condition.

For over four hours, Adam had not moved from the laser. He had even had his lunch brought in to him. He was watching every part of the process and he was now ready to bring Joy back to full size. We had so many questions to ask her. Adam said he was ready and everyone agreed to bring her back, so Adam reversed the ray, drawing her back to her full size. She was growing by the second into a full-grown woman. Adam pulled the last trigger and she appeared, but as she turned, we could see her face was still not totally formed. She turned towards the wall, hiding, as she knew she was not completely formed, then turned again. This time, you could see her face coming together.

It seemed it was the last piece of the jigsaw puzzle, and as her lips materialised, she started to talk.

"I'm back! Am I alive or in heaven?" Joy asked.

"You're alive," Amanda said, "and it's great to see you again."

Joy said, "Yes, I'm glad to be back. Would I be able to have my money now, please?"

"Yes, of course, but can we ask you some questions first and check your vital statistics before you leave?"

"Certainly," Joy replied.

Everyone was heaving a sigh of relief; this had never been done before and Joy had come back in one piece which showed we could now move into space travel, having conquered this new milestone.

We could trust the process of shrinking used on our participant and she had come out well. It did not mean there would be no repercussions in the future, but, for now, we were on track. We were all willing to risk the ray. Joy had shown us the way... she had been rewarded for her sacrifice and had left with no ill effects. Only time would be able to tell that what we were doing was science fiction. Shrinking a human being and being able to bring them back to normal size alive and well had never ever been invented or replicated anywhere; to our knowledge, this was a first and if we never made it into space, just this alone was an accolade every one of us could share.

Now, we would all have to go through what Joy had endured to reach her goal of funding her child's operation. We were now going to be the risk-takers and chance miniaturization to reach the outer limits of space – those opportunities we had all talked about were now possible. It would be a selection process of who would be the first to make the journey into the unknown and we would have to just pull out all the stops and go for it. In the morning, when we all met, we would have to refine how we would be able to travel using our minds to transport us to other worlds and galaxies and eventually be able to transform ourselves into other beings, entering their minds and living amongst them in a way so macabre and presently unknown to humans.

Chapter 9

———— ⋅ ————

A door had opened into a stratosphere of mystery and endless opportunities to further the power of the human brain, projecting human technology beyond any limitation to broaden the sphere of the brain to levels never before encountered. Our knowledge as we know it would seem primitive. We were all going to have to take the leap if we wanted to be part of the pursuit of excellence. We were going to show the world our achievements in space exploration, exceeding the boundaries known to man. All of us were becoming excited as we got closer to the pinnacle of our space travel. We were ready for our minds to take over and propel us through space at lightning speed.

We all had already got through the mind zone, where you can meditate enough to move objects. That would allow us to transition our brains into trillispeed and travel at speeds faster than the speed of light. By working together, using our minds in unison and focusing our thoughts at the same time and place, we would be able to exceed this speed by who knows how much. The timing would have to be impeccable to ensure we all travelled at the same time and speed to reach our destination. To begin with, we would only be going a short way to get used to the speed we would be travelling at. Our intention was to go around Mars first – a round trip of 158 million miles – not too far in the scheme of things.

It would give us time to think our way back before going further afield. We could explore Mars before we went further; we needed to know what life forms existed in our galaxy. There might be a dead planet with no oxygen to breathe but we would still be able to have a look as we travelled around it. We had to get there first, so we were now going to have to get ready to be shrunk to enable us to leave our planet and propel ourselves into space and beyond.

We would have to synchronise our brains to ensure we communicated and travelled as a team. Mutual thought processes and telepathic understanding were the only way we could keep in contact with each other. We would also have to find a way to learn more about our brains to build a force that could repel predators or invaders – a type of mental barrier we could use to warn us of impending danger so that we could defend ourselves.

We were working with the idea of being able to project a beam around us to imitate another life form. Savarnee and Amanda were currently in the laboratory working on a solution to a process of maximising transformation to enable us to imitate and fool other entities that we were one of them; that would allow us to move freely between the entities and learn from their knowledge and infiltrate their world for the benefit of ours and to use their knowledge to define the dimensions in other galaxies and universes. This was an exciting time in our lives. We were hoping that we could have the ability to imitate and intimidate any threat we might encounter during our voyage, allowing us to travel through the galaxies to discover new worlds and entities in relative safety.

We would not be as well placed without it and we needed to have as much protection as we could possibly acquire. It would be a perilous journey for us all. We could not take physical weapons as they would not be able to travel as matter… only the thoughts from our minds would take us to new worlds. We would have to train our brains to send the telepathic messages to upload our minds with information being created in a surreal world of the soul, mind and spirit. All messages would be transmitted between the mind and brain at lightning speed as we searched for new horizons.

Nothing appeared now to be beyond our imagination – we would be able to access the whole dimensions of space and time. The minds would have left our bodies; the bodies would only be vessels to come back to when the mind needed recharging. There would be no need to come back for food or water – as long as the bodies were suspended, that would keep the brain alive to ensure safe passage back. We estimated the mind would increase its capacity at an alarming rate on every mission, and there were no boundaries to the capability we had discovered. We would never think in a fifth dimension again.

Racing through time and space was not an easy concept to comprehend, but this was an unbelievable supernatural experience which was going to rewrite the history books for the next 5000 years.

We all needed the protection to enable us to take the leap we had created. Savarnee and Amanda's brains, when synchronised, had a wireless connection moving between them at light speed like Bluetooth. The connection could not be broken by somebody walking between them as the speed the signals were travelling at was faster than light itself, and to break it could cause a catastrophic imbalance to both of their brains. It had to have uninterrupted telepathic transfer.

Chapter 10

————◆————

As well as the speed of our brains being well in advance of normal activity, we had also discovered how to connect our brains wirelessly and make them work as a team, sharing information between us in a wireless internet. Fibre internet was no longer an option for communication; we had left that dinosaur behind, and now we were at lightning speed. Information was passing between us in a billisecond and getting faster every time we connected.

We could now converse and understand each other without even talking, just by using the mind. It was processing information faster than we could comprehend – the speed of contact was at another level – a split-second thought was becoming lightning-fast information to the receptor. It was as if it was out of control. It seemed impossible to be able to increase the speed any faster, yet as the signal left one of us, we were getting faster at receiving it and the amount of information was staggering.

We could decipher the words; now were changing to a light-speed digital morse code which we understood. It was taking over normal thoughts of a fourth dimension and the signals between us were now coming in a digital form of code. Our brains were translating the code back to speech in a flash.

We were now talking in a sixth-dimension code and our brains were communicating between themselves. We would have to try and slow down; with all the information going between the brains, they were creating a potential overload. They were now learning how to connect to each other and were searching for others to connect to. We did not want the technology going outside the team, so they were in another stratosphere searching for information. In a former life, had we been from a planet that had evolved beyond the spectrum of intelligence and burst out and come to Earth as prehistoric cavemen?

Could this have been the answer to some of the anomalies that we did not understand – how they built structures or the knowledge they had whilst everything was prehistoric around them?

Amanda broke the connection with Savarnee. We were both tired, as the information that had come between us was absolutely staggering. Amanda was recapping the information that had travelled between us. We confirmed that the information and the new code the mind was creating were the same. We both confirmed to the team that the connection and information was perfectly flawless and could not be faulted. We were going into a new dimension where the mind, brain, soul and spirit were working together. The brain was moving on into another world, creating a whole new digital dictionary.

It would only need what we used in the fifth dimension for reference back to primitive times. It obviously knew it needed to move on from language into another sphere of knowledge. Our worry was whether we could control what we had, or could the mind take over the brain completely and take control away from us? We had to ensure the brain stayed in control of the mind and would only use it when we sent signals to it from the brain. The words were broken in places between digital and English language. The brain was starting to also define other languages – French, Spanish and Russian – the words all being transferred into a digital form that only the brain could decipher at present. The chain of conversation was at an end for the moment but sections of the brain which were previously never used were now becoming active.

We were talking about the limits of the brain, if there were any, but there seemed no end to what it could create.

It was faster and more powerful than any computer; everything was at trillispeed. We were all astonished at the results of the connection between the two brains. They had taken over creating and talking to each other. They were in the process of creating a whole new language and translating all the languages of the world with it. Just to be part of this was absolutely amazing. If we were doing this now, what would we be doing when we got into space and were connecting as we travelled? Would we be able to connect with alien species and have conversations with them? Had we come that far? Would we be able to time travel?

Everything seemed to be open for debate and we were all excited about the journey in front of us. Savarnee and Amanda now had that connection we all needed to see to ensure we could fully communicate between us. There would have to be no possibility of losing each other in space. We had to know it was all future-proofed as there would be no room for error. We simply had to make sure the mission was a success.

We would all have to go at exactly the same time so nobody was ahead of or behind the others; our brains would have to synchronise with each other and propel us into space at a billispeed. We would be travelling too fast to be able to stop and look for a lost soul in space. We each had to be looking after the whole team and not crusading somewhere on our own. We needed to be in the security of the many.

Chapter 11

———◆———

There were still a lot of precautions we would have to take and it was not going to be a maverick operation – flying by the seat of our pants was not an option. Propelling atoms, what we were deemed to be, travelling at billispeed, although virtually invisible, we were going to be an entity to be recognised as we had the ability to travel at well beyond light speed should we be pursued by alien species. Although we could increase our size to match any other species, we could not be measured as matter and were merely images mimicking the new species we had encountered. We would be able to transform back to the size of atoms in an instant.

We would only be able to be tracked by the propulsion trail left in space but we would be gone, light years away by the time they found it. The speed of travel was unimaginable; our weak spot was if they could catch us in a vessel of some kind whilst we were mimicking an alien species as we would represent the species in a mass but were vulnerable to capture when at full size of the species around us. We would have to be careful when we used our mimicking ability as it could work against us and could end our space travel. We would have to prepare ourselves well as there would be no light in space; just a dark view into the unknown. We could only navigate our travel by the planets and the suns in their solar systems.

There would be no need for artificial light as we wouldn't be able to see due to the lightning speed as we navigated the planets, unless we decided it was of interest to us to stop. We had discovered the secrets of life and time and it was our mission to conquer it all. There would be no going back, but we would have to make sure that wherever we ended up on our adventure, we could get back to our bodies to replenish the energy source to enable us to keep travelling and exploring new worlds, mapping out routes and places for generations of future travellers to discover.

If we could tell people what we were about to do, they would never believe it – our mission would be top secret with no boundaries. We were looking for a benefactor to fund new technology as we were not geared up for exploration and our remit was limited to research only. If we were going to keep pushing the boundaries, we needed proper funding but we did not know who or how to approach the prospective funders. For now, we were going to go it alone and fund what we could manage as we had the equipment we needed to go where we wanted to go. However, we all had greater goals we were looking to conquer in the future. We could not keep funding from our own salaries, even though it would be worth anything to be on an adventure out of this world. Discovering galaxies and universes beyond, we would be unsurpassed in our quest to discover new worlds and species not previously known, but we could not be sure what we may encounter on our travels.

I shuddered to think what we would encounter as we travelled at billispeed into the unknown – only God himself would know what was behind that curtain of darkness and it was now our turn to discover what had been hiding since our time on Earth began. We were on our way into a totally new dimension… the world and the universe were our oyster and we were going to see it out to the maximum.

We would go down in the history books for eternity – no explorers before would ever be able to measure up to the pioneering mission we were now going to experience and who knew what perils awaited us? Tomorrow was going to be a new day. Savarnee and Amanda were going to be connected by their brains' Bluetooth and hopefully be able to work out more of the digital language as a telepathic signal to communicate. Without it, we could not converse at the speed we would be travelling at. It was imperative that we had ticked all the boxes before we got ahead of ourselves. After all, it would only end in disaster if we were not completely ready for transition to atoms. We had to be able to find a route back to our bodies for our return. There were so many things to think about that it would not be done overnight.

We had all agreed not to rush in where angels fear to tread. We were overexcited when Joy came back to full size with no apparent problems but we had no more information on how she was now. We'd had no contact with her so her condition was not apparent to us and it would now be our risk to stand in front of the laser with Adam on the trigger. We would just have to hope he wasn't having a bad day and he overshrunk one of us. It was all too much to think about although the excitement of going into space was phenomenal. We were also wondering if we would be able to travel the way we envisaged we could. Would our brains be capable enough to shoot us as atoms through space into our intergalactic sixth dimension with all the knowledge we encompassed? Would it be enough to get us there to new worlds? Maybe the whole idea would turn out to be an apocalyptic nightmare. We had to have positive thoughts – onwards and upwards we thought; let's see what happens.

We had a schedule set for travel. Adam would stay on the laser whilst Anthony, Savarnee and Amanda would be the first to go. Blaise would co-ordinate the mission along with Adam whilst the others were projected into space at lightning speed. We could not move yet as we needed the digital language to be complete since we could not communicate without the digital code. If we travelled too far before we lost contact with the rest of the team, this could be a disaster. A digital transmission would go millions of miles more than a radio signal. We had to be thinking in the sixth dimension; we needed to forget the first five dimensions. We were now in undiscovered territory where we could not relate to anything and call it the norm. There was no more norm; all that norm was now history and we were in the future.

Chapter 12

————————◆————————

We were possibly a new species of transformers, able to reduce size, mimic other foreign species and travel at unimaginable speeds. We had become supercharged beyond the understanding of the human race; we were so far ahead of any country nobody anywhere was even thinking on our wavelength. We were totally tuned into our intergalactic travel and we were now as close as it gets to going. Could we be leaving intergalactic trails across the galaxies... roads to follow for potential invaders of the Earth?

We would have to try and cover our tracks to avoid leaving too many clues about where we had come from and where we were going. Had we done enough safeguarding to venture into the unknown? Everything we did was the unknown. We were risk-takers, masters of what we had invented, and it seemed nothing was beyond the remit we had set. We had all decided not to stall the missions anymore but to go full steam ahead and turn our dreams into reality.

We all knew the risks and we had to go the extra mile to realise them. We were going to confirm or reject all the predictions professors had made about the galaxies. We would soon have the secrets of the universe in our hands; the world would never be the same again. We could be up there with other species travelling around space, intergalactic voyagers.

All bets were off; we would be just atoms in a universe of diversity awaiting to be discovered.

We were due to go after the weekend. It was now Wednesday so two more days at work, then we were set for around 11 am on Monday morning. Adam would be behind the laser doing all the last-minute tweaking and Amanda and Savarnee had the digital language virtually complete. They had both worked well together – there seemed to be a real connection between them. Their brains synchronised perfectly and they were deciphering the codes well and creating the digital language we needed. Adam, Savarnee and Blaise had created a digital map of our galaxy marking all the planets, the black holes, the stars that were going to be visible to our naked eye as we passed them or connected with them at short distance – some gateways might not have been visible from Earth.

We were looking for new life that existed beyond the gateways in the abyss of space or within the enormity of the gateway itself, possibly leading the way into a supernova of planets and other ancient galaxies. We might encounter toxic places where life does not exist, torpedoed into a supernova of implosion and explosion creating a no-go zone for any life form that might have lived there or wanted to. Space might not be as clean as we imagined it to be. There could be carnage and debris caused by a supernova destroying life, as Earth could implode one day creating meteorites floating through space on their own mission to collide with other planets or eventually burn up. Who knows, one of them one day could have Earth stamped in the very fabric of our previous lives; parts of our Earth becoming threats to other planets in a solar system far away. Would this be our destiny, one day to be a threat to other planets, caused by our wars and neglect of Earth through our greed and ambition?

We were creating our own toxic world where only machines could exist above ground and we might be the witnesses of our planet's destruction where machines keep us alive on the surface, whilst we grow superfoods to sustain life below. As we would have to have our physical bodies with us, we had not got to a stage where we could travel to another planet that could accommodate our need for oxygen and the range of gases we breathe to keep us alive, and we would not be able to live without a form of matter to propel us into outer space. This was not going to be available for hundreds of years to come; the technology was not here to enable long space travel.

We would be able to navigate by the stars and planets; there were trillions of stars lighting our way into outer space. There was also a form of sun-like planet evolving into a radioactive show of light-burning gases forming a super-bright star to be seen and adored by stargazers in a moonlit sky some zillions of light years away, burning in a twinkle as a diamond in the sky. Could we even reach the closest star in our travels or would we be restricted by our body's brain to shorter trips to nearby galaxies? We were reaching for the stars and were going beyond our dreams to reach the end of our galaxy and into others, virtually touching some of the stars we see shining in our skies.

Man had long dreamed of going to the stars, however, he might not have been too keen to go if he had known what stars were, just burning gases in an explosion of atomic fire, too toxic to even approach to examine the makeup of the gases and the purpose of its existence within the solar darkness around it. It seemed they had been put there as a beacon of light to show the way to new horizons, but only time would tell the story of why and how they evolved and what their purpose was.

Chapter 13

————— ♦ —————

With the weekend fast approaching, the whole team seemed excited but apprehensive about the outcome of the shrinking. Adam was trying to make us all see the sense in what he was going to do but Amanda, Savarnee, Anthony and Blaise were not so forward in their support for his method. Still, it was the only way it was going to happen. After the shrinking, when we took off into space, we did not know if we would be lost in the darkness, floating around looking for adventure or a way back. Although Amanda and Savarnee had indicated the brains had a digital homing program installed that could lead them directly back to their bodies, this had not been tried and tested and was only an addition to all the other mind-blowing information they had created. Between their minds, they had been creating all the information that could be transferred easily once it had been fully synchronised.

We could transfer by telepathy, with a new style of language, and speed of transfer was instant… so fast it could not be measured. We would have to levitate our bodies to the horizontal position to connect with each other for all the information to transfer. We were not sure why we had to levitate and remain horizontal but nothing actually worked if our bodies were not in this position. Lying horizontal seemed to slow the metabolism down and put the energy into the brain, the body seemed relaxed, and a good flow of energy existed between the whole team.

We were going to share information in the morning so we would all have to connect. We would be informing security that we were doing some highly classified work and the doors were going to be locked for security purposes. It would not be good if they came in and all of us were levitating two metres high in a room. At first, they would think there was no gravity in the room and we were floating like spacemen without suits. It would be difficult to explain to our superiors why the hell we were all floating around the room, and more to the point, how we came to be floating. We would not be able to explain ourselves so better to be safe than sorry.

I thought there would be periods of up to two days where we would be in space. We were not sure how we would be able to explain why we were always behind locked doors; we could not transfer the machinery to any other locations as it was not ours to transfer and the equipment was worth millions of dollars. We were going to have our mission times as holidays so as not to attract attention to what we were doing. We would never be allowed to continue if we were found out and it would then become a military affair and we would be in a secure unit and have no freedom to carry on our missions.

Everything we wanted to do would have to be approved at the highest level; we would not be able to let our minds run free. We would be virtually incarcerated in a secure unit, every single action accounted for. There would be no rest again as the military would make sure they extracted every morsel of knowledge we had amassed, along with the real work we were directly employed to do. We had created a fine balance between our work and our exploration into other worlds and the unknown. Our adventure was about to start; things would never be the same again. It was an explosion of apocalyptic travel with no boundaries. A voyage into galaxies never discovered with the best telescopes known to man, and nothing could see the distances we would travel to.

The worlds we would encounter in an intergalactic sphere of endless space created by an apocalyptic supernova the size of Earth, fragmenting into galaxies far away forming their own universes, diverse to the species that lived on the planets and endless in their structural tenacity holding on to the end of time. Our thoughts were on Monday and the mission for the three – Amanda, Savarnee and Blaise. They had gone home early; they were going for a drink together just to make sure they had destressed ready for Adam to pull that trigger on the laser. It could literally be their last weekend on Earth but they could be under the earth if it all went wrong. They had all gone to a restaurant for what appeared to be 'the last supper'; they were going to enjoy the night together.

When they next saw each other, they would be standing in line to be shrunk, an experience only tried by one person – Joy; nobody else had even tried it out. It was going to be a team effort but nobody wanted to go first. I thought if it didn't go well, the others left would be backing out of the experiment and the journey into space. They had come so far; they were here now and there would be no backing out. Everyone was committed but drawing the short straw was the old way of setting the order of shrinking. The one who drew the short straw would be first, the middle size second and the third… well, they got to see the other two go first.

Still, there would be no time to examine the first two subjects before the third went to meet their fate.

Blaise said, "Not to worry; as if a star fell out the sky, it will be a fait accompli."

Amanda said, "Typical of you to talk about something like that whilst we're trying to get over our nerves! Would it be fair if Adam burned us to toast?"

We had to think positive that it was all going to go well if we were going to enjoy the night. Blaise asked if anybody wanted toast; it didn't go down well with the others.

Blaise was laughing and Amanda punched him on the arm and said, "There you are – that was 'armless."

Anthony was there laughing and so was Amanda.

Blaise said, "Well, I suppose I deserved that. Let's get on with our meals and think about cremation."

Amanda stood up. "You are joking now, aren't you?"

"Yes," Blaise said, "it was my turn." Amanda said, "Next time, you will be wearing your dinner!"

Even Anthony laughed at that one. It was all in good humour and no offence was taken.

They were all a bit on tenterhooks; even Blaise, the joker, was not too happy but time would tell come Monday morning when they were stood in front of the laser. They wanted to draw the straws on Monday so as not to upset the weekend too much. No one wanted to go under the laser first – not even joker Blaise, despite all his jokes, so they all decided to stop talking about it and move on and enjoy their meal. Blaise spoiled it again by saying his steak was burnt and overdone; not what the other two wanted to hear. It didn't go down well, but again, Amanda managed a condescending smile.

As soon as we ate our food, we decided it was time for an early night and to enjoy the weekend. We paid the bill and went our separate ways, sharing the same message to each other to enjoy the weekend, take care, and we would see each other on Monday morning. We all went home to spend time with our loved ones as it might be the last time we saw each other for a while. Where we were going was not for the faint-hearted and it would take a lot of nerve and courage to do what we were going to do. Who in their right mind, or in desperation, would stand in front of a laser and be shrunk to the size of an atom? On the flip side, it was going to be an experience and most of us believing in fate, we were ready to go.

We wanted to be 21st-century explorers, but it was slightly daunting to think what we might find on our mission. Monday would come fast and we had committed; the only thing that remained unknown until Monday was who would draw that short straw and have to be shrunk first. We would be on a journey to a place where trillions of stars lit the way in a never-ending adventure, travelling as atoms, returning within hours, sometimes to be enlarged back to our normal selves and levitated to allow regeneration of the atom, and then we would be off again. We would try to keep our journeys short for now until we knew we were all communicating properly in our new digital language and were managing to find our way back with our homing function. It would be impossible to travel out of Earth's orbit without this working.

Amanda and Savarnee had said it was working well and giving out a pulse signal they could recognise; the brains were so powerful in their creative phenomenon and we needed all the knowledge our brains could create. The amount of information the brain could create was unreal and it was instrumental in creating the new digital language. How could this be? Had our brains been in another dimension before this, another world, another being? The possibilities were endless. How could they do what they were doing, yet they were creative in exploring new ideas? The telepathy between our brains was second to none, so there would be no holding us back. We were already in another unexplored dimension where no one had been before.

Chapter 14

———◆———

Monday came round fast, and before we knew it, we were meeting in reception. Everyone was present —nobody had bailed out; a full house.

We were all ready to go.

Blaise said, "My nerves got the better of me and I haven't slept much."

Savarnee was indecisive on whether he was ready or not. Amanda said she was ready but was hoping she didn't draw the short straw.

Anthony said, "Well, I'm good to go so draw those straws. I'm ready to obliterate you all!"

Nobody laughed at that. It definitely was not funny. The three of them had nerves that were jangling. I don't think any of them were ready to transform from between five and six feet to the size of an atom.

They all had the jitters as to who would pull the short straw. Anthony got out the straws and made them all level at the front; he was going to offer them. Amanda went first. The straws all looked exactly the same, so she did not know whether to work from left to right or from right to left. She pondered as her hands went close to the straws, really apprehensive about picking one. This could be a disaster as life was everything and death was final. Could she find the courage to pull out the straw from Anthony's hand?

She looked around and could see beads of sweat on Blaise's forehead as he was looking at the straws. There would have to be a coin toss if Amanda picked the long straw. It was a nervous situation and Adam made it worse by fooling about with the laser, moving it around and pretending to fire it at us as we stood there.

He was just being a bit mean pretending he was zapping everyone. I don't know what he was laughing at – it would be his turn soon. There would be no escape for him or Anthony; it would be their turn to be tormented into a procedure which, although tested, was not really suitable for space travel as we knew it. We were all interested to see the outcome of the shrinking, but no one wanted to really take part in the experiment. However, we realised we could not move on without the initial procedure to shrink us ready for travel. Although Amanda had voted to pull the first straw to get the competition moving, she was also hesitant to pull the straw. Amanda knew it could be the end of life so she lunged over and grabbed the straw. It seemed to come out of Adam's hand really slowly. I think he was being himself and putting pressure on the straws so they were harder to pull out.

Eventually, Amanda jerked the straw out; it seemed long and Savarnee and Blaise's eyes popped as they saw it. Had she drawn the short or the long straw… maybe the one in the middle? Deep down, Blaise and Savarnee were hoping it was the short straw but it looked too long to be the short one. Amanda seemed to heave a sigh of relief – hopefully, there were no straws longer than hers. Beads of sweat were now running down from Blaise's forehead onto his face. Adam tossed the coin and, as he caught it in his hand, he swapped the coin from the palm of his hand to the back and covered it with his other hand.

"Ok, boys," he said, "call it." Savarnee shouted 'heads'; Blaise had been too slow. Adam took his hand off and there was the coin with the heads up – it would be Savarnee's choice of the last two straws.

Savarnee, born half-American and half-Jamaican, with his skin shining as the sunlight came through the window, wished Blaise all the best as he made his way over to Adam who was holding the last two straws. Adam smiled and wished him good luck as Savarnee put his hand on the left straw. Amanda was looking on in fear as the straws could be longer than hers; she would have to be so lucky for them not to be.

Anthony said, "Don't worry, Amanda, I think you're up there with the long straw."

Savarnee was about to pull the left straw but something made him change his mind. In a split second, he pulled the one on the right. As he pulled it, the straw came out fast… it was only just in Adam's hand… it had to be the short straw. He stood there holding it in his hand. He could not believe how short it was and they could see a nervous look come over him.

He looked like he had seen a ghost. His golden skin was turning a lighter colour. Blaise's face had a sigh of relief on it. He had a feeling the straw, although possibly being shorter, would be a real long shot for Savarnee.

"He should have stayed where he was on the left and not switched it," Anthony and Amanda said to each other.

It's like being in a queue in a supermarket and switching to one that seems to move faster – you always leave the best and switch to the worst as there is always someone holding up the queue you switched to.

Blaise had to draw the last straw. He was more confident now and he was good to go and went over to Adam to draw it. He looked confident and pleased that Savarnee had drawn the short straw. He went straight over and put his fingers on it and pulled it. He nearly fell over… he had drawn the shortest straw! Savarnee was off the hook – Blaise was going to be first to be shrunk.

What a disaster! It taught Blaise not to count his chickens before they're hatched. He looked devastated – the clown of Friday night had brought on his own destiny to be the first in the team to be shrunk. He could not believe it would be him. This calm, relaxed, funny guy was about to be shrunk to virtually the size of an atom. He was shaking as Adam asked him to stand in front of the laser. Amanda and Savarnee, his co-travellers, helped him over to the laser and stood him in a large tray up against the partition wall. The tray was there so that they could identify him when he was small and to contain him until he was ready to travel.

Adam shouted, "Look up!" and as Blaise looked up, Adam zapped him; he went so fast and virtually disappeared. Savarnee and Anthony moved the tray and emptied a small item onto a stainless steel trolley in the middle.

Blaise would need the space to grow again; he would have to be suspended on a bed of air from a small fan we had invented. We would all have to follow the same routine. This would only keep him suspended there until his return from space. It seemed strange but it was what worked and could be the way to future space travel for everybody who wanted to push the frontiers forward in venturing to other worlds never seen before. The danger was that now it was possible to shrink a human being, what would be the effect on life expectancy if going on regular missions? People would be thinking about either not being able to get back or shrinking having a disastrous effect on the body causing sudden death.

It was quite gruesome thinking about the possible outcome of short-term travel into space; nobody knew if we could even be shrunk twice. What kind of person would come back? Would they even come back complete or would they be lost forever and never return to the body waiting for its host?

Adam's trigger finger was getting itchy and he was pretending to shoot at the walls and ceilings, which was making Savarnee nervous. He was between a rock and a hard place; his life was on the line. He was wondering if it was all worth risking his life for – it could be the end of Savarnee as we knew him. However, he knew he could not claim the glory if he refused to go; it was just bad luck that he had drawn the second-shortest straw. He would have to make a decision fast – go or stay – it was going to have to be a split-second decision. Walk or run, sink or swim, jump or die… it made no sense not to go so he stood in the tray in front of the wall.

"Do it; ride or die," he said. "Do it fast," he shouted to Adam, "before I change my mind!"

Adam pulled the trigger and Savarnee started to shrink. He was one of us, not some stranger like Joy, and he was shrinking before our very eyes.

We were all shocked; even Adam was astounded at how fast he was going. He would soon be virtually invisible to the naked eye. For some reason, good or bad, he had shrunk smaller than Joy; he was nowhere to be seen. He was just a speck, the size of a pinhead, and could only be seen using a magnifying glass. Someone would have to pick him up and put him onto the table ready for his return.

It was now Amanda's turn. She was sweating – all those days of drinking and having fun would be gone in a second. There would be no more night-clubbing and dancing days; they were going to be over now. She stood in the next tray.

"Here goes," she said to everyone left.

"Goodbye!" Adam said.

Amanda said, "That's not nice; it's like I'm not coming back."

Adam said, "Don't worry; your life is in my hands."

Amanda replied, "Exactly! That's what I'm worried about!"

Adam said, "Stand up against the wall. I'm Billy the Kid and you're going down."

Amanda laughed out loud and said, "It's your turn soon!"

She was still saying it as she was being shrunk. She just started to disappear into her tray. It was so quick; like the laser had been turned up and was vaporising them all faster than ever before.

Chapter 15

————◆————

We hadn't checked Blaise, Amanda or Savarnee to see if they were ok and that was a mistake. Since they were late being shrunk, they would have to go into space today. They would go around Mars, a mere 160 million miles away, for a round trip. Adam and Anthony bent down to look in the three trays with a magnifying glass and a microphone. All three of them seemed to be active in the trays.

We asked individually if they were ok and they replied, "Yes." So, it had been successful... Adam had given them the correct dose and they were all in good health.

We needed to put them on the trolleys so they could be ready to go. They would have to synchronise their brains to be able to download digital language, levitate and go on their journey. Their minds would now leave their bodies and start the journey into space. They were too small to pick up so Anthony suggested letting them crawl onto a piece of white paper.

"This?" Savarnee said. "It will be too high to climb without a ladder."

Adam laughed. "It's so funny," he said. "They can't even climb onto the top of a flat piece of A4 paper."

We would have to think of something smaller in height that they could climb onto.

Anthony said, "We have surgical scalpels… they could climb onto them then we could drop them onto the paper." We could see them as a black mark and they wouldn't be harmed. We had to make sure we did not lift the scalpel too much whilst they were on it. What would seem a fraction to us could be a twenty-metre drop to the paper for them and that could be catastrophic.

Later, we would have to think of other ways to transfer. Maybe they could stand on the middle of the trolley, then there would be no need to transfer them.

Adam said, "It would not be a stable environment for them."

We would have to think it through before the next shrinking.

"Especially as it's going to be me and you next," said Anthony.

Adam said, "Yeah, we don't want any broken bones before we go."

Anthony said, "Well, let's make sure these have got no broken bones before they go; it would be difficult to treat someone that small. Microsurgery would be out of the question for an operation – we haven't come that far in medicine yet."

"That's an area we must explore," said Adam.

Anthony said, "You have quite enough to do on working the laser and shrinking your colleagues without inventing instruments to repair atoms."

Adam laughed. "Yeah, I can see where that's going; blaming me now so it's my fault if they fall off the paper and break their bones."

Anthony said, "Well, we didn't see that one coming; we best get it sorted or there will be trouble for us all if they come back injured. It's going to be risky if we bring them back with broken bones as we don't know how well they will arrive and mend afterwards. We can't make any mistakes; we will have to deal with it as we see it. We need to put them all in one area and get them to synchronise their brains so they are ready to go."

Time was of the essence. The idea was to circle Earth and take off in the direction of Mars. It was 80 million miles there and 80 million miles back, which seemed a long way in 10 hours. Their brains had synchronised and they had the digital language installed into their brains. The co-ordinates had been set and they were ready to go.

Amanda said, "Our heads are buzzing and we are ready to fly!"

Blaise said, "Open the window – we are ready."

Savarnee said, "I'm bursting for the toilet!" They all burst out laughing as everyone had spoken at the same time.

Blaise said, "I'm ready to go, I can't wait."

Amanda said, "I'm going to count back 3-2-1 and we go on one. Synchronise now… 3-2-1 go."

They all left in a flash of light. There seemed to be a vapour trail as they left the room. Adam grabbed the binoculars and shouted out in excitement,

"Can you see them, Anthony? They're like stars twinkling in the sky. They are in formation; I wonder who is at the front and who their wing commanders are. They are flying in a V-shape. I want to know who is leading the team; they're virtually on the edge of space."

Anthony said, "I can see their trail on the telescope. I'm going to try and track them through the Hubble telescope. I've managed to hack into it so I will have control of the space telescope for the next ten hours. I have sent a fault message to the computer so it will be ours now whilst they are trying to fix the software, and by the time they get to diagnose what's wrong, we will be back safe, then I will reinstall the space telescope.

The times we are going will upset their clear views, so they will be sending up rockets to mend it. We have to hack it as they will see the perfect formation going through space from Earth and will try and track where the vapour trail will lead them. It will lead them back to the laboratory and we will all be in big trouble. They will put us on trial and lock us up and throw away the key when our prison sentence is served."

Adam said, "Wow, never thought about that, the cost of sending up a rocket to fix it when it was our meddling that caused it to go offline. I'm sure we would have a heavy sentence to serve afterwards for taking the Hubble satellite telescope offline."

Anthony said, "I can see them now – they are on a latitude line circling the world. They have just passed the Hubble now and they're on course to do what we agreed – once around the world and if all is ok, set a course to Mars. It will be more visible from space; they have their co-ordinates to get back so it's a quick trip around Mars and a straight path back to Earth."

They disappeared from the view of the Hubble telescope but it would be literally seconds before they had rounded the Earth. They would be on a course for Mars and would discover more in a day than the scientists had found out since time began. It would be something so special, not even seen in a film taken by a space rocket sent to find out if there was life there.

The team would discover what was there or what was not there, flying at beyond lightning speed. They would be back in less than 10 hours. We had estimated them doing it in between 6-7 hours but had allowed 10 hours for any diversions or problems along the way. Adam was now hooked onto the Hubble telescope and he had transferred the footage to a large screen in the laboratory used for identification of the galaxies. We were focused on looking out for them.

"There they are!" Adam shouted. "They're just a flash of light. I can see them over there, look."

"Yes, I can see them," Anthony said. "There they are; three lights in the sky. I really wish I knew who was taking the lead. I bet it's Blaise."

"No, definitely Savarnee," Adam said. "It won't be Amanda – she has no sense of direction; she has trouble finding her way home."

"Let's have a bet – I think I'm on a sure thing that Blaise is heading the team," said Anthony.

"No chance," Adam said, "definitely Savarnee. He wants to be at the forefront of everything he does."

Anthony said, "No way! It will definitely be Blaise. He knows all the co-ordinates and he is good at finding places. Let's make it $100 to win then… you on for that?"

Adam said, "Let's see. I can't see them on the screen… I'm losing them… they are too small to see. Perhaps in future they could leave some kind of trail so we could see where they have been as they're passing."

Anthony replied, "Oh yeah, a trail for somebody to follow like a path in space, ha."

"I suppose you're right," said Adam. "Someone could trap us if they found a trail of vapour or a line of lightning. They would have to limit the speed as lightning would leave a trail as you went through the light barrier. Just like thunder at the speed of sound."

"Wow," Anthony said.

It seemed really slow… a snail's pace. The fastest speed we humans had ever achieved was 17,500 miles an hour, in space, circling the world in orbit. Speed now was being defined at beyond lightning speed… virtually unmeasurable. No instrument from Earth could ever measure the speed we were now travelling at. This was record-breaking technology, beyond even the dreams of man. Nothing would ever match it for a thousand years; we were so far ahead of our time it was unbelievable.

Chapter 16

———◆———

We were moving the boundaries all the time. The team was a tight one, all working together in a synchronised approach. We could see no limits to our capabilities to conquer space. Three of the team were now on their way to Mars, but Anthony and Adam were wondering how far they had gone. It had been an hour since they rounded the Earth on a path to Mars. We could clearly see the planet but not the team. We listened for some communication; we couldn't understand why they had not sent any signal back to us. Between them, Amanda and Savarnee had created a digital language only we could decipher. The digital code was too fast for anybody to translate without the receivers from our synchronised brains. There were no electronics; just signals transmitted from each other's brains. We were all connected in a five-way conversation.

Adam shouted to Anthony, "Got a signal at last!"

Anthony said, "Yeah, I heard. It's Amanda who is transmitting. She said, 'We're around 3 hours away from Mars.

We had problems with the formation we were flying in and have gone through a space cloud and the static electricity caused by space dust was affecting our transmissions. We will have to stay out of them in the future and try and divert around them. We have seen so many things on our travels so far. You would never believe what's out here; it's amazing.

The whole of space is an abnormality you could never believe. Although we can't see some things, we feel them out there, not speaking and invisible to us, but we feel them as we pass. Like spirits, they have a presence, lost souls darting about around us as we fly past them. It's fantastic – an immaculate conception of space'."

Anthony said, "It sounds wonderful. I can't wait for my turn."

Adam said, "Me too. Blaise, are you there?"

"Yeah, I'm here."

"How is the team? Are you heading it?"

"No," Blaise said, "Amanda is. She is fantastic with directions. It's a good job she came on the mission. We wouldn't swap her for the world."

"I will second that," Savarnee said. "We are acting as her wingmen. We are flying now beyond speed that we can't believe existed."

Adam said, "Wow, I can't believe it."

Savarnee said, "What, the speed?"

"No," Adam said, "that Amanda is heading the flight."

Amanda said, "Get me! I am cruising! It will be your turn next to be my wingman."

Adam said, "Really? You're sure?"

"Without a doubt," she replied. "Anyway, got no time for you earthlings – we're off. I'm going to take the speed to the next level and see if we can set some new records up here in the abyss of space, where there is no final frontier. This is the start of an adventure that will go down in history, and we could be leading the force for colonisation of other planets."

We could see what planets were suitable for human life to exist in the event of a collision from a meteorite or nuclear war between the aggressors and the defenders. We would have to make provisions for evacuation to a planet we could identify as suitable. Our mission was just one of a trial run; we would not be looking for a rescue planet at the moment. We would be concentrating on rounding Mars and getting back to Earth safe and sound.

"I will witness that," said Savarnee.

"Me too," said Blaise.

"And me!" said Adam and Anthony together.

We were all synchronised and we could hear thoughts as well as speech.

"We're with you all the way," Adam said. "Good luck."

Amanda said, "Yes, I will come back to you if we have a report of UFOs or any other matter. We are going to round Mars just to check for any forms of life."

Adam said, "Try and land and have a look around for life."

Amanda said, "No, we might not be able to get back into space. I'm not sure about static electricity; it could break contact with our bodies. We can't risk it so early in the flight but we will go around and see if there is life or if it's a dead planet. I will report in… I estimate… two hours based on our speed now. We are not going to increase speed because we were cruising at a safe enough speed for us to be able to see what was coming around us as we ventured into the unknown. Nobody has physically seen the dark side of Mars… in fact, no human has physically seen any of Mars, the light side or the dark side."

It all went quiet until Blaise said,

"We have an unidentified vessel on the port side travelling 360 degrees northwest at trillispeed. Shall we slow down and investigate it?"

"No," Amanda said. "How long has it been tracking us?"

He said, "Around 12 minutes."

"Thanks, Blaise," Amanda said. "Let's pick up the speed to half trillispeed and see if the craft follows us. Still keep your tracker on. Blaise, let me know when it's gone."

Blaise said, "It is obviously not capable of our speed and we must have been like the old days of miles per hour when the supercars would leave the boy racers standing."

"Yeah, I will go for that," Savarnee piped up.

"Well, let's get on with our mission. We can drop back to billispeed as I can see we are not being tracked anymore, but whoever it was, we have to be cautious. We need to be aware they are there and could return. We don't know their capabilities but we don't want to find out too soon. We need to be able to round Mars and get out of here. It could be a patrol craft and we could have alerted it to our presence. Also, we have to take that course on the way back. Did you have the co-ordinates, Blaise?"

"Yes, Amanda."

"Well, when we get back near them, let's increase speed back to half a trillispeed and hopefully fly past so fast they won't know we have been there. Keep those co-ordinates in your head after we have rounded Mars and let's put the pedal to the metal and get the hell out of there. Are you there, Savarnee?"

"Yeah, I'm here on your starboard, right behind you, Amanda."

"Good; Blaise, everything good?"

"Yes, Amanda, in line with Savarnee and everything ok; no problems here."

"Good. We are coming into Mars' orbit now, so let's go and do the perimeter. Once around and gone, keep a lookout, boys, for any signs of life."

"Ok, Amanda," Blaise said.

"Same here," Savarnee said.

Amanda said to the team, "We are good to go, so let's do it; let's hit this and move on fast. We have a schedule to keep and we don't want to be late on our return so let's get around. Keep a good lookout for any craft or beings hiding on the dark side of the planet."

Then to Adam, she said,

"We're entering orbit around 8 miles away from the gravity of the planet. I can feel it pulling us in."

"Ok, Amanda, just be careful you don't get too close – it could drag you in."

"Ok," Amanda said. "Come closer, boys; you're too far behind me; close up."

"Ok, Amanda, we are on it, just wasn't paying attention."

"Good," Amanda said. "I have to make sure we all get back safe; we don't want you venturing into unknown territory alone. On your own, you would be isolated and an easy target, so we have to stay together. We are strong as a group but weak on our own."

"Ok, team leader, got it," Savarnee and Blaise replied.

We were on our way around Mars. It was bigger than the Earth but not by much so we would take about the same time as circling Earth so we could map our way home timewise.

"Keep your eyes open, boys, for any signs of life," Amanda said. "Try and stay in formation."

"Ok, team leader, our eyes are on it."

We had come in on the light side of the planet. We saw no signs of life as we moved over the top of the planet, then all of a sudden... "There! Over there... I can see some kind of spaceship. It's a large one... wow... where did that come from?"

Savarnee said. "Let's go and look."

Amanda said, "No, not yet; let's track it all first. Get the co-ordinates and, when we have fully checked Mars, we can go back and investigate the spaceship. It could be one of ours from a mission."

"No way," Savarnee said. "It is too big; it is a monster. I only caught it out the corner of my eye, but it was enormous! Nothing like that has ever left Earth."

"We heard that, team," Adam said.

"Yeah, me too," Anthony said. "It sounds exciting."

Amanda said, "Yes, we will have a flypast if we meet nothing else on the planet whilst we go around. Keep your eyes open, boys, well… your senses peeled, but more important, keep in formation."

Chapter 17

———————◆———————

Savarnee said, "I can sense signs of activity, like buildings on the starboard side. There has definitely been life here. I can see buildings that look deserted but I'm sure I saw some kind of spaceship near them, half sticking out the ground – looked like it had crashed, team leader."

"Ok, let's have a look."

We turned back to the position where Savarnee saw what he thought was a spacecraft buried half into the area near the buildings.

"We can see it, team leader. It is a spaceship, but nothing like we have seen before; it looks abandoned. They could have been on a mission to Earth when they crashed on Mars. They must have made some temporary buildings, by the look of it. There does not seem to be any life there now. We have seen no signs of surface water or clouds, so unless they lived without water, they must have perished there. The dust looks like it's been there a long time. Let's fly around 2000 meters above and just check if there is anyone alive or if they all perished."

"Ok, let's go," Amanda said. "Follow my lead."

"Yes, team leader," they said as they entered the perimeter of Mars.

We were all excited to see extraterrestrials if they were visible. We were the ones on a test mission and we had to get back to base.

"No gravity here, boys; we're straight in," Amanda said. "Right, follow me. We will do a flypast; keep your eyes peeled, boys. If there is life, they are fairly advanced to be here, so just make sure you're not too close for them to fire at us if they have any weapons."

Blaise said, "Wow, something has just erupted from the planet's surface; let's get out of here!"

Amanda said, "Let's go! Let's get the hell out of here; go, go, go – trillispeed, all of you. Forget the rest of the planet – let's get as far away from here as possible. Don't look back, guys, let's just head home fast."

"Base here," Adam said. "What's happened, Amanda?"

"We have had something fired at us… not sure what it was but it came close. It's time to hightail it back to base. Our ETA is around 3 hours."

"Ok, team leader, as soon as you can."

"Definitely!" Savarnee said.

"I will second that," Blaise said. "I will be glad to be home; space isn't quiet or as dead as we thought. We need to make sure we have some kind of protection on us for future missions."

The team were coming again tomorrow, or in the future, one day.

"I suppose we might have a weapon," Blaise said. Adam and Anthony would be the wingmen and Amanda would be team leader on the next mission. Blaise would be in reserve for any illness to step in straight away. It would not be safe with only a team leader and one wingman. Whoever it was had been notified of our arrival and would be looking out for us, so we were no longer on a Sunday outing.

We would be encountering another species from other worlds; it would be too much to take in at such an early point in our mission but it was there – we may have to alert the authorities at some point to our discoveries. Possible invaders could be based close to Earth. They were only a step away if they were part of an invading force. If so, how many were possibly hiding under the planet's surface away from the view of our satellites? They could be awaiting more craft to come ready for an invasion of Planet Earth. It seemed nobody was aware they were here so it would be inevitable that an invasion would take place soon. They were not hiding around the other side of the planet for nothing.

Why would they live in virtual darkness when they could live in the light? Could the object that came from the planet's surface be some kind of rock from a volcano erupting below the surface? We needed to check it out on the mission tomorrow. We could not leave it to guesswork. Whatever it was came up with some force and had scared Blaise into bringing it to our attention. There was definitely an alien species down there as we are still launching rockets into space; no one on Earth had the capability of creating a spaceship like we had just seen. It could only have been a disaster or a major fault with it to have crashed and burned half of it into the planet's surface.

Our thoughts were everywhere. We agreed we would go in early tomorrow to discuss what we had seen and decide whether it was something reportable. It was fairly quiet on the way home; we didn't know for how much longer with what we had just noticed on Mars. We would be able to keep it to ourselves. We may be contravening the law on reporting what was on Mars, although we could not confirm whether it had come from a rock spewed out from a volcano under the surface of Mars or something that had been fired at us.

It was too much of a coincidence that a volcano could erupt and throw out a physical rock as we were passing over. We were three twinkling light flashes; it was more likely we had been tracked as we circled Mars and they were ready for us. It could not just have been a coincidence. We needed to go back and make sure that they were not a threat to us on Earth. None of us were sure why they had come to Mars and if the spacecraft was actually damaged or if they were living under the surface in tunnels. Perhaps the spacecraft had been left there deliberately to allow the crew underneath to have access to the outside.

Maybe it hadn't crashed but was like that for a reason. Although now we had the ability to reach out and arrive at other planets, one of the problems we had as Earthlings was that we had no ability to go to war in space. To send a rocket to Mars would take far too long when fighting a war with an invader. If we could only find out what they were there for... could it be they were just passing through? The reasons they were there could be unlimited but our thoughts were that they were an attack force from another planet.

We were now coming into the range of the Hubble space telescope. Adam had turned it back on as we went out of range, so it was now going to have to go out of action again so we were invisible coming into Earth's airspace. Our problem was that other space telescopes might see us but not be able to identify what we were. We decided to break formation so we were not so recognisable.

Amanda said, "Break; let's go in separately."

"Ok," Savarnee said. "I'm going in."

Blaise said, "Me too."

Amanda said, "Good luck! I will be behind you; see you there."

That was our call to go straight in. It was getting dark and we were more visible going through the clouds into the laboratory. The trolleys were in place and Savarnee went first, straight in through the eye of his shrunken levitated body.

Chapter 18

————◆————

Adam was on the trigger, so the moment he saw Savarnee enter his body, he started growing on the table. This was a better way than Joy had; at least they were not standing up. It hadn't been a good position to be in when being enlarged back to size. Blaise came through the window and straight in, so Adam zapped Blaise and he was on his way back. Amanda was the last into her body – everyone was back to normal size with no ill effects. The expedition had been good… no adverse problems from the shrinking. Everyone felt well so there would be no need for any treatment. This was a good thing as we would have a job at Accident and Emergency at the hospital explaining what had happened.

We were definitely flying a kite and we would be in trouble and people might be there investigating us to find out what we were doing in the laboratory. We were all ok so we would have to deal with it if it came. We had decided that no one should go into space more than twice a week to minimise the risk of overdoing the laser and having a reaction. We would not deem it to be safe until we had travelled enough missions to satisfy the team that there were no lasting effects on shrinking a human being. We finished our meeting and it was time to go home. It had been a long day... being shrunk and doing around 175 million miles in around 9 hours was not too bad... just a walk in the park.

You could say we had a long day ahead of us tomorrow. We all wished each other good night and parted until the morning. Tomorrow would be another day, another discovery, another world.

Time was going so fast – no sooner had we arrived home than it seemed like it was morning again and we were all in the laboratory. It was the turn of Anthony, Adam and Amanda, who would be team leader again. We were ready to go. Blaise would be performing the procedure as he had been trained by Adam on how much to pull the trigger on the laser so as not to overdo the procedure. They were now waiting to be shrunk; we had broken the code between the protons and the neutrons that are a part of the makeup of the atoms. We had managed to break down the barrier between the electrons that encase them that stop the process of shrinking with any form of instrument like a ray.

The ray would have to be able to shrink without heat to avoid burning. We had created the ray nobody else had ever made; it was possible to sustain life even during shrinking. There was no heat at all – everything was at room temperature so we had the perfect combination. The team had been shrunk and were ready to go; all the systems were in place. The team were synchronising their brains ready for the journey. Amanda gave the thumbs up that we were ready to fly, Blaise opened the window and they were gone in a second.

The Hubble space telescope had been taken offline ready for the flight they were on. Amanda was team leader again with Adam on the starboard wing and Anthony on the port side. They had taken off at billispeed, one and a third times faster than the speed of light, so they disappeared faster than the eye could see. We caught them heading on a course for Mars before they disappeared in the abyss of space.

"Team leader to wing commanders, can you move up? You're too far behind. Close up, please," Amanda said.

"Yes, team leader," Adam said.

"Ok," Anthony replied, "copy that, team leader."

Amanda said, "Ok, boys, that's where I want you so you can watch my back. Keep all eyes peeled for any craft that could be following us or making a flank attack on us. We never know what we might meet, so we will circle Mars but take another route, just to see what's on the other side. I don't think it's a good idea to show the aliens on the planet our source of energy today. We need some kind of weapon, even if it's projected and not real. It might be enough to keep an alien force away. We have speed on our side… we could virtually go beyond trillispeed, one and a half times faster than the speed of light, to get out of trouble. Let's get round here fast, boys. I would like to take a look at Mars to make sure we are not missing anything on our space mission. Then let's go and check out Jupiter and see what is hiding there. It's only another 80 million miles there, but keep a lookout for anything dodgy."

"Ok, team leader," Adam and Anthony replied.

"Let's go," Amanda said. "We are going to increase to full trillispeed."

"Let's see what our brains can do," Adam said. "I've never seen so many stars… the sky is alive with them. It's unbelievable just how many there are; I'm in a maze of them. I think this is what they call lost in space. It's like a needle in a haystack trying to find our way through the shooting stars and meteorites darting all over space."

It was all out here to see. It was beautiful in its form but it made you wonder what we would find on our way to discovering the universe. What danger would we run into? I could not see it being an easy ride. We were bound to run into the unexpected. It seemed like a calm sea we were navigating, with strong undercurrents that we had not yet encountered but were there just waiting to swallow us up and drag us to the bottom of the abyss of space.

We could see millions of stars like grains of sand on the beach, a ball of fire generating heat like the nuclear core in a reactor in a nuclear power station; two forces fighting each other for dominance and producing fierce heat, light years away. They were fireballs of gases in other galaxies thousands of light years away and we were passing them at beyond lightning speed yet the further we travelled into the vastness of space, the more we could see. We made our way into the dark unwelcoming depths of the unknown, three small objects travelling so fast the naked eye would not be able to focus on us; we would be virtually invisible.

As we passed the stars, they seemed like pinheads on a football field, and space was awash with them. We could see debris from ones that had burnt out and had started to break up and float in space until they could find another atmosphere to burn up in or disappear into the vastness of space.

"Base to team leader," was transmitted.

"Team leader to base," Amanda replied.

"Are you on course for Mars? We haven't heard from you."

"Yes," Amanda replied. "We're on our way to Mars to just check it out to see if we can scan it for any activity. We have to know what we are up against in our galaxy."

"Ok, Amanda. What is your estimated time of arrival?"

"We should be there in around two hours; we can see it. Well, strangely enough, we passed a rocket on the way around a million miles away – that must have been the one Earth sent recently."

Anthony said, "Well, you didn't show us!"

Adam said, "I didn't see it either."

Amanda said, "It would have been beyond our sight in seconds. It will pay you to keep your eyes open and stop daydreaming, both of you. We are looking for extra-terrestrials and you two are dreaming away. I wondered why we had no contact between us – you were not paying attention to where we are. In the future, you will both be team leaders and have to lead a team on longer, more involved missions."

"Got it," Anthony said.

Adam said, "I have a feeling we are being tracked."

Amanda said, "Ok, let's change direction, keep the same speed and let's see what happens. I can sense them now; we have something to your rear starboard side. Let's find out what it is. Let's break to port on my command… Break, break."

We all turned to port.

"Keep formation," Amanda instructed, "and stay on my wing, both of you. We need to take evasive action. Team leader calling base."

Blaise answered, "Base here."

"We are being tracked by an unknown object. We have to investigate now before it fires on us."

"Ok, Amanda, your call; deal with it."

"Ok, boys, let's go. Follow me and keep your eyes open for extra-terrestrials."

"I see it!" Adam shouted. "Let's get it."

"No," Amanda said. "Get it with what? We don't have anything to fire at it. We can't even give it a warning shot. Ok, we're on it; let's flank it and get behind the craft and see what it is."

"Ok, team leader," Anthony said.

"Same here," Adam replied. "Let's track it, keep formation and let's try and scan it and see what it is. Whatever it is, the vessel is clearly not from Earth, so what is it and where is it going? Let's stay on track behind it. Have you got that, base?"

"Yes, confirm your position, team leader."

"We are around 1.5 hours away from Jupiter on a level track. We are just approaching Mars, heading directly on a course to pass on the starboard side."

Chapter 19

————•————

"Ok, we are tracking the spaceship. It appears to be like a V-shape in its form and travelling at billispeed. We are following around 50 miles behind; it does not seem to have noticed us. I would say it's about the size of a football field. It's fully rounded with no sharp edges. We must have taken it by surprise; it looks more like it's some kind of cargo spaceship transferring... could it be some type of prison ship?"

But why would it be travelling so fast and where is it going? Had this species found out how to move matter at this speed? Our rockets, doing 17,500 miles an hour, were not exactly fast.

The spaceship was definitely on a course; it was set on some kind of autopilot because whatever it was, it did not seem to be manned. It was on a fixed course and staying on its track, not veering away. It was easy to see how you could transport items around the galaxies. We could see we were light years behind this race of beings that could build this spacecraft in matter then just cruise the galaxy at billispeed. It was so far ahead it made no sense.

"Drop down behind the spaceship so we're not so visible," Amanda said. "I'm sure it knows we're here. It would have to be futuristic with its communication and transmissions and receivers to be able to go where it goes in such a mass; it is enormous in size and travelling at fast speed."

We were coming up towards Mars. It looked fairly barren; we could see the surface was not blue like the Earth. This indicated there would not be much water unless it was under the surface, but there seemed to be some things built there. We think it had sustained some form of life at some stage in its history. The spaceship was not stopping. We had called it Voyager as it was on a mission to somewhere; none of us knew where. We would have liked to follow it but it could have travelled two galaxies away or more. We now had to focus on Mars and what there was there.

As we rounded it, we could see it was really cold on the north side as there was a frosting on the planet.

"Base, there is some kind of water vapour taking place, possibly mist or cloud causing water vapour to conden-sate and freeze during the night and possibly vaporize during sunlight." There would not be too much heat as we were getting further away from the sun – the further we explored the colder it was. It might get warmer as we encountered stars or bigger suns in other galaxies.

There could be thousands of galaxies waiting to be discovered and who would be waiting there to welcome or destroy us? We had so far to go and so many discoveries to make… it was exciting but daunting at the same time. We were in a groundbreaking era and we were making leaps and bounds into the unknown and we had even witnessed an alien spacecraft carrier. We were starting back around Mars; what else could we take back? Only what we had seen as we rounded Mars 335 million miles away from Earth.

We had come so far in no time at all. We could see Jupiter far in the distance, more than any other planet as it was so large; it was a beacon in the sky to follow. It was visible 385 million miles away from Earth, but it was awesome to see the planet closer. From Earth, it would have taken up to eight years for a rocket to reach it, but we were almost halfway there in less than twelve hours.

We could only see the planets on the way to Mars. We would not see them as we passed; they would just be a blip of light shining as we passed on our journey. We had scouted over Mars; it seemed there was no activity that we could see and we were going to be on our way back to Earth. As we rounded Mars, we could see Earth only 335 million miles away.

Mars was a strange planet in its format; it seemed to be flat and uninteresting. It looked like it might be able to sustain some life as there appeared to be water vapour clouds around it stopping some vision to the surface, like a dense mist. It was a bit eery and quite scary. We could not see what was below and it seemed to be divided into large patches of around 1000 miles per cloud, almost like a farmer's field defined in its area. It was only half the size of Earth but it was a mysterious planet – the patches of mist were possibly a cover for what was living underneath it, but why the strange patches? They were not symmetrical but patched like an old pair of jeans, however, they appeared to have sharp lines and corners that could lead us to believe they were being projected there to either keep out the rays from the sun or some kind of protection screen that could be dangerous to others.

Time was running out and we all had to get back. Adam and Anthony would now be working on overtime; it would have been a 14-hour day and they would not be happy.

Chapter 20

———◆———

We were on our way back, billispeed all the way. We needed to put millions of miles behind us... what a way to travel, we all agreed.

"Pull in closer, boys," Amanda said. "We need to stay in formation – we can't afford to be separated. We have to all get back together in one piece... well, three pieces."

"Ok, team leader," Blaise said.

"Same here," Savarnee replied.

"Ok," Amanda said. "Let's get hyper, let's go."

"Ok, with you, let's go," came from Savarnee. He was a bit of a maverick. He wanted to go as fast as he could but Amanda had it all under control. She was leading and no one was moving off her wing, including Savarnee the speed machine. He would have to throttle back a bit. We were on a mission to get back as no one knew how long we could be out of our bodies and how much energy we had used.

It was as much of an unknown as the areas in space we had been exploring. We could not be overdoing our remit to have a brief look around. We had travelled millions of miles, but if we had sat down in front of somebody else and told them our story, they would have laughed their heads off. We were in space and had travelled vast impossible distances in half a day. As we were nearing home, Amanda sent Savarnee a code to close up.

"Savarnee, you're drifting again. You have to keep the team intact as, without a wingman both sides, we are vulnerable to attack."

"Ok, team leader," Savarnee replied.

"Good," Amanda said. "Make sure you don't let the side down again. We need you back alive."

It was the last leg of the journey to Earth. We were calling it the blue planet – as the sun came around, we could see the blue oceans, but it looked so small in comparison with Jupiter. We had to make tracks and get back to base. Earth now looked so inviting and so visible with its blue oceans and green fields and trees. We could see Earth but needed a direct line, so we used our homing signal connection to the brains in our suspended bodies. We were entering the ozone layer so just about home. Amanda sent a mind message to Adam to open the window for entry back to our brains.

We would have to be lasered again back to full size; none of us was looking forward to that laser. We had no idea what it was going to do to us long or short term. We were coming in towards our city limits; Anthony had interrupted the satellites to get us back in. We flew straight through the window in formation. Savarnee was where he should have been for a change and we landed in front of the laser. We were just about twinkling in the room waiting to be absorbed back into our bodies; it would only be one laser each to join our bodies. We just hoped it would work and not be like Joy, although once our bodies were complete, they had to be activated by laser to grow again.

We needed to be able to get to a place where we could leave our bodies as an atom and be able to return to a full-size body without the laser but we had to be shrunk to allow travel from the bodies. We all recovered perfectly. Blaise seemed to be a bit jerky but soon stood up on his own.

Adam said, "He's been like that most of his life!"

Amanda and Anthony laughed. Anthony said he had a bellyache as he was laughing so much; it wasn't a good welcome back for Blaise. Adam was on form. We would have to have a meeting to discuss the day but we had come in too late. We should have left Mars earlier and not stayed to observe the spacecraft as it might have been going to another galaxy or universe beyond our capabilities.

Whatever it was, it was far in advance of us to make matter go that fast without burning up. They must have had a heat-resisting compound to make them able to travel at fast speeds between galaxies. We decided to call it a day and we all made our way home; tomorrow would be another day. We were excited but tired, but we decided we would have our meeting in the morning. Adam and Anthony had kept the workload at the laboratory in check so that if we had an inspection, everything would look like we were all working for the company in the jobs we were employed to do. There was no time for slacking; we would have a job explaining ourselves with 3 bodies lying suspended over trolleys.

Our actions were beyond reasonable behaviour; we had gone way beyond our remit. We would be lucky to work again anywhere if we were caught. The only consolation was that we were rarely visited and the security personnel had no clearance to enter our laboratory. The doors were always locked as our work was classified and not accessible without authorisation, so we were reasonably secure. We had a tight unit so nobody spoke outside the laboratory.

All being well, it would be Adam and Anthony on the wing of the team leader tomorrow. We had to make sure we had not got any visitors coming to the lab – they very rarely came without an announcement a week before as long as we were producing results for our work. We had accelerated our work and were only releasing some parts every week to keep the company happy, so they were not suspicious of what we were doing elsewhere.

It would be a short night – it was gone 10 pm and we had to be back in the lab at 9.30 am at the latest. Adam lived the furthest away, so he would be coming back before he went! Time would have been better spent sleeping on a trolley in the lab rather than going all that way just to sleep and get up early to come to work.

The morning came around fast as usual and we were all tired but ready for the day. We had a meeting about our paid work, and what we were doing but we were well ahead of ourselves as usual. Adam and Anthony were keen to get off. They had been briefed on where we had been and what we were going to explore on our mission today. We got ready to go through the procedure as normal – well, I suppose it wasn't normal but it's what we had to do to travel. We would be going off at 10 am as planned to get maximum time into the mission. We were going to search beyond Mars to see where that spaceship was going but it would be a journey into the unknown, perilous if not controlled.

We'd had a bad experience; we didn't want it to be repeated elsewhere, at least not until we had a way to fight an aggressor. We would have to be vigilant in where we went and make sure we were safe; only speed would get us out of trouble. Looking back on the spaceship, it was well beyond our technology and it would have been equipped with weaponry possibly better than anything we had on Earth. This solar system didn't belong to us, but to other beings far in advance of us who were able to carry cargo or people through galaxies. They were not to be underestimated.

Chapter 21

———◆———

We had all gone through the shrinking and Savarnee had opened the window. All Blaise had to do was block the satellite and Hubble telescope so we could not be seen by eye or by radar. We were ready;

Amanda said, "Let's go," and we were off.

"Stay with me," she said as we sped into the atmosphere.

At last, Anthony and Adam were off with Amanda. They were at Mars within one hour. Amanda and the team were all communicating well. Amanda was now the expert of the team and leading it.

"We will be on track to do a few more miles today," she said. She hoped, if time permitted, to scout the planet looking for alien species.

Adam said, "*We* are the alien species, not whoever we find; we are in one of a million galaxies."

It was infinity – it seemed there could be no end to it. The darkness of space was lit by shooting stars and the sun, now more distant than ever as we travelled. There was an eery feeling to space, so vast and empty, like the deepest oceans, black and mysterious. You know there is something down there but dare not go for fear of the unknown. We were similar in space – there was no starting point and no finish. It was just the vastness of it all that made it scary.

You wanted to wrap yourself up in a blanket to feel safe in bed, but there were no beds here… just three atoms flying at billispeed on our way to discover new worlds we had never encountered. We were looking for planets with water to sustain life, but what life? What if they didn't need water to live? We were just a rogue outfit of scientists and we might encounter them sooner than we thought.

We were coming up to Mars and Amanda messaged everybody.

"Good; we are here," Adam and Anthony replied.

"Right, let's move a little faster," Amanda said.

"Ok, team leader," Anthony replied.

Adam said, "Shall I lead the way?"

"No," Amanda said. "Stay on my wing; this is my command."

"Ok, team leader," Adam said and we continued as we throttled up to beyond billispeed.

We were travelling faster than lightning and leaving a trail in space behind us. We were not sure what we were leaving behind; it looked like space was burning up behind us.

"Close up," Amanda messaged. "Let's keep things tight together. We have limited time to do…"

"Wow!" shouted Adam. "Look at that!"

"Yeah," Anthony said. "It's just gone behind Mars; it was fast."

Amanda said, "Ok, I will finish what I was saying later. Let's go and see what it was. Stay together – no maverick missions, boys. We go as a team. It's going to be hard to tell someone if you get lost in space. Let's go and see where they have gone. We have to be careful as we are vulnerable. Whatever it is was not doing our speed; it looked a lot faster – possibly trillispeed. We have no chance of catching up with that vessel. It was possibly a spaceship. Can you see the trail it left? It's like a road burning."

It was as fast as a laser beam of light. We accelerated around the port side of Mars, and as we came round, it was really black as coal. However, we could see light shining in the distance. We flew towards the light.

"Don't go any further!" Adam said. "We can't follow as it's gone into a gateway and there could be more than one spacecraft there. There must be at least two so we have to get out of here fast before we become vapourised by them and they are able to detect us."

"Yes, I agree," Amanda said. "Are you ready, Anthony?"

"Yes, team leader. Let's get the hell out of here before we are discovered. They are far in advance of us and we will not be able to defend ourselves. We don't want to be captured by some alien species. We haven't got a clue what they would do with us but being this close, they must have seen Earth. We are only 300 million miles away."

Adam laughed; it was strange to hear somebody laugh in digital language.

We needed to move fast and get back to earth as we were not equipped to deal with any foreign invader.

Anthony said, "Foreign invader? That's us!"

"Yes," said Amanda, "but I meant us coming up against an entity we have never encountered before. Come on, boys, let's go and get out of here."

We were doing well – it seemed the brains were keeping the digital communications in line with the speed we were travelling at so we could converse with each other at trillispeed. We were not sure what it would do at higher speed, but as long as we were in a proper format, in the not too distant future, we would be able to use digital communication like Bluetooth. Nobody was straying into a zone of no communication.

"Team leader to base," Amanda transmitted.

"Yes, team leader," Savarnee replied.

"We are heading back. We have seen spaceships travelling into a gateway at speed far in excess of ours. There seemed to be more than one, like there was a base beyond the entrance. We are making our way home."

"Ok, team leader," Savarnee said. "Stay safe and get home as fast as possible. We have an inspection in the morning so we will have to cancel flights until further notice."

"We will be back in around one hour," Amanda said. "Can you disable all satellite telecommunications and block the Hubble telescope? We don't want to be seen approaching Earth."

"Ok, team leader," Savarnee said. "Blaise is doing it as we speak."

"Ok, base," Amanda replied. "We're on our way home."

Blaise opened the windows and, five minutes later, in came the team. Right away, they were lasered and back to size and ready to work. It had been a short day due to the alien presence; what were they doing there so close to Earth? We needed to inform someone that there were extraterrestrials hiding in a gateway behind Mars but we were sure we would be dismissed as if we were making up stories to draw attention to ourselves; no one would believe us.

Chapter 22

———◆———

We couldn't understand why the Hubble telescope had not picked up on the spacecraft going
in behind Mars. We all believed it could possibly have
looked like a shooting star; our thoughts were running
wild because there were extraterrestrials close to us. Were
they there in the gateway for a reason or were they planning an invasion of Earth? They were definitely far more
advanced than us; would we be food to be harvested by a
population that saw us as a food source planet?

We could simply be theirs to meet their needs, never
cultivating, just devastating planets of their species, leaving
them barren and nothing more than wasteland. We had to
inform the authorities they were there. But on the other
hand, would it cause them to ask too many questions? That
might put us in a predicament if we had to say where and
how we had come by all the information we had. We had
put ourselves between the devil and the deep blue sea.

We had to think clearly about what we were going
to do. We would have to get the meeting over tomorrow

and put some plan in place ready for the next mission. We had the inspection; we had progressed in all the right areas for the company and excelled in others. We worked as a team and dreamed as a team. We wanted so bad to be the best at what we did and would not relinquish the work we were involved in.

Space travel was paramount to the program; we had agreed between ourselves to discover the undiscovered, hopefully to the benefit of mankind. We would now have to be protectors of the Earth. Nobody else could go where we went and we could reach places never ever dreamed of. We could all say we were the dream-makers; we would be the saviours of the world, not the mavericks. We would be able to scout the galaxies looking for threats to our existence. We would be better pre-warned, or at least we would be able to try and defend ourselves if we knew what was coming and what force they would be bringing with them. We would have to meet and plan our strategies. We needed laser weapons; we were not strong enough to repel a full invasion of Earth.

We were on our way home; we had been checking if there was anybody following us. We had a clear way back but our thoughts were going through us like knives through butter. We were approaching Earth and would soon be back at the laboratory.

We had to stay on the planet for a while, forget space and make the weapons we needed to defend us and Mother Earth, which gives life to us all. An alien invader could destroy Earth, so we had to be the ones to protect it. They were out there and we would have to try to protect against any aggression from alien interference and possible annihilation.

We were going to work on some sort of weapon we could use against an aggressor but we would not be able to transport it as we were atoms. The weapon would be matter and that technology would not be available possibly for the next 100 years, if not longer. However, if we could adapt the laser to track us to meet a potential aggressor, we could message back the course they were now on, and their co-ordinates, and then we could laser them from Earth or from satellites with the ability to carry the lasers. We could probably be able to destroy the spaceships before they got into Earth's orbit. They might not be coming here to invite themselves to a party, so it was our thinking that forewarned is forearmed.

We were not going to be caught sleeping as an invasion was taking place. We had to use the team to its full ability to create a substantial weapon to deter them from entering our atmosphere. We decided to get started straight away, but we were not sure how we would explain to the company what was happening. We would have to spill the beans to tell them what we had been doing and how we knew what was happening outside.

In space, the vastness of it and the lack of light to see other species would make them obscure to any telescope. They would have total cover of darkness to lead a surprise attack; the human species might cease to exist. Whoever they were, hiding in the gateway, they were there for a reason. We had to go back and look at the flotilla of space-craft they were amassing. At least we would know what to expect if they were there for an invasion.

The questions we asked were why they had not landed on Mars – a closer planet? Why were they hiding down a gateway? Did they have some kind of base there where they could meet and communicate with a mother ship, as they do in the oceans with naval ships when all the captains anchor ship and meet at the naval flagship that usually has an Admiral on board? We seemed to have a gut feeling they were not there to transfer cargo, and the way the spaceship darted across us, it was questionable, to say the least. Our duty now would be to make the laser. We had the best team and we all agreed we would make the laser a deadly weapon of war.

There would be no time as the invasion could be imminent and they would be on our planet within months.

They were too close for comfort; we were hoping we were wrong and they were there for different reasons. We had a busy week ahead of us. We obviously could not adapt the laser immediately but we had the ideas on what we would have to do to make it into more of a weapon.

We would have to be able to use it here. The laser was a formidable weapon, so we were hoping that we could zap any invading aliens from Earth.

Chapter 23

————◆————

We were in deep trouble because we could no longer see light any more. If they came into the Earth's orbit, how would we even know their intentions? They could be friendly and we could start an intergalactic war with aliens not knowing the outcome. We had no remit to do anything; we were mavericks without any authorisation to do anything. We had to be ready since no other country was close to what we were creating.

It could be another holocaust, us rounded up and exterminated by an alien power, created through us working and living in America for a pioneering American company. There would be no rest until we had a weapon that would be effective against an invading army. Our success came from our free spirits to do what we wanted, to let our minds run free to create and build. We felt our team was the best in its field and could not be compromised by some bureaucrat coming in and shutting us down. We would have to have some backup just in case.

It could all turn into an apocalyptic nightmare. We had assessed the speed of light and nothing else would be more deadly than the laser travelling at 186,000 miles per second, equating to trillispeed, faster than any eye or telescope could see. Instant power from a deadly weapon – we had the technology to adapt ours, however, we did not have a license to create anything like this and doing so would bring us a long custodial sentence. We would probably never see the light of day again; we at least would have to share the responsibility between us. If one was caught, we all would be; there would be no mercy shown but it was a risk every one of us was willing to take.

We would be going back to Mars. It was closer to Earth, as it is 335 million miles between the Earth and Jupiter. In the morning, we would find out if it was a couple of random spaceships or whether it was an attack force. Amanda voted herself to go but we all agreed three missions in three days would be too much. We needed her here to help us with the laser with Adam and Savarnee and Blaise would be the ones going on the mission to Mars.

The gateways were sometimes an entrance into other galaxies. They could not land on Jupiter – it was just gases around the planet – unapproachable for landing and there could be a million galaxies, endless through space to discover and we now knew we were not alone. Why were the spaceships going behind Mars? They were alien beings and we were only just tipping the sixth dimension. There would be perils to come along with an adventure too amazing to think about from where it was starting to where it would finish.

Tomorrow would be busy and we would need our thinking caps on. There would be an American team going to Mars tomorrow with Savarnee, a Jamaican American, Blaise, Amanda and Adam who were born-and-bred USA citizens and Anthony who was Canadian American but lived now in America. They would be instrumental in the development of the weapon.

When we arrived back in the morning, Anthony said he had sat out all night on the house decking thinking of ways to adapt the laser; he had a lot of thoughts to relay back to the rest of us.

Savarnee and Blaise were getting ready to be shrunk by the laser. Amanda was chatting to Adam about his thoughts on what she was thinking about.

Adam said to her, "You need to move as you will be shrunk as well as them."

"Ha," Amanda said, "you always have to pull the rabbit out the hat and you have to make a joke about everything."

"Just quick-witted," Adam replied. "Are you ready, boys?"

"Yes, we're ready."

ZAP! They were atoms.

"Open the windows, Amanda," Adam said as Amanda opened the window. Anthony was working on blocking the satellites and the Hubble telescope.

They were off on a spying mission; they could make Mars by 11.30 am. Adam, Amanda and Anthony had been left in the laboratory to work on the laser. We could not have it out of action as, when they returned from the mission, we could not reverse the shrinking without the laser.

There were so many unknowns... would altering the laser give out large amounts of energy, too much to be able to change back to the same level needed for shrinking and reversing? We could not afford to get it wrong or the laser might disintegrate the team. We needed another laser – one we could adapt as the weapon, the other to keep for shrinking for our space travel. Blaise and Savarnee had passed Mars and were approaching the back of the planet. They had contacted the team to let them know they were only minutes away from scouting the planet and were on the starboard side about to round it to the port side where the gateway was.

"Just at the helm off the portside, we can see the gateway," Savarnee relayed back. "We're going down in seconds."

Back at base, they had no signal from Blaise and Savarnee; they were in the gateway. We could only hope they were safe. It had been two hours since they had gone into it and still no word. Could they have been captured or destroyed in some kind of chase through the darkness of the gateway? There would be no sunlight to light the way – only the dark shadows of Mars and the sunlight bouncing off the front of it. They might just be able to get a glance at the light bouncing off the starboard side of Mars if they were to come out of the gateway they had gone down to draw them out.

We were now concerned – over three hours had passed – they would not answer us or transmit back. Would they even return? They were just an entity travelling through space on a mission to where… we had no plan. We were just out to discover new worlds and cultures.

Still no word from the boys; it was over four hours and time was running out. We could not launch a search party as we had no way of getting them back or defending them from an invading race. We would have to just wait and see what would happen. We were hoping and praying they were ok.

Chapter 24

———◆———

"Team to base," Blaise was transmitting. Wow! Everyone heaved a sigh of relief. "Everything good here; we are just coming out the entrance passing Mars. We have some light at last. We have travelled so far down that gateway but it's endless in its size. There is life here… we don't know where… we were trying to find it but we had no line of sight for a signal so we were effectively lost in space. We were not sure how to get out; we were flying by the seat of our pants.

We had to go with a gut feeling to travel out of the gateway. There were no markers anywhere that we could use to navigate ourselves out of there. We were lucky there were only space travellers darting in and out of areas. There was no sun to guide us but they must have had co-ordinates to where they were going." Savarnee was talking all the way back about the life in the darkness of the gateway and the fact that the amount of traffic in space was not what they expected.

There was no invading force waiting in the winds for an invasion – everything seemed to quiet. Mars had no spacecraft on it; everything looked empty and lifeless. We would not have to make too much headway with creating the laser; we could take time to do this later and get it right first time. We could concentrate on space travel to see what's really out there as a threat to the Earth. We seemed to be the only real blue planet in our galaxy with large surface water areas. Well, actually, 71% of Earth's coverage was water and 29% land so it looked so inviting to invading sources; plenty of room to hide in the depths of the large oceans.

We would need to create a laser that could travel virtually wherever we went. We could give our co-ordinates to base and they would be able to use the laser in a split second on attacking forces, or a calculated strike if further away, as long as any of the team could break free. We could obliterate the capturing force and free our team. We would never be able to take weapons into space as we had nothing but our brain cells to communicate and drive forward to our discoveries.

A high-pitched tone would be used as a distress signal from one of us but used only in extreme emergencies. It would be an alert transmission built into our digital language. We would only have to think it to give the co-ordinates and zap them. The program on the laser would be able to calculate the distance, longitude and latitude before firing to fry all aliens posing a threat. We had come from a warring planet; nothing good was coming for the aliens from Mother Earth.

We were approaching the start of the gateway and the rear of Mars to round it back on a course to Earth.

"Hey, look at that," Blaise messaged Savarnee and he picked up.

"Yeah, seen it, Blaise; two spaceships just darted into the gateway; good job we're out. I don't think they saw us but let's get going before they come back. Let's round Mars and then trillispeed all the way back to Earth. I'm surprised they didn't spot us or sense us on their digital sonar or whatever super sonar they had."

"I'm glad," said Blaise.

Savarnee said, "Well, I'm sure we could outrun them."

Blaise said, "Don't be so sure of that – did you see what speed they were doing?"

"Yes," Savarnee said. "We could outrun them."

"Ha!" Blaise said. "Well, we might see one day soon. Let's see if you can outrun their laser when they see you."

"They must have been on some kind of autopilot to miss us as we were right at the side of them as they were entering the gateway," Blaise said.

"I really want to have a look back down there again. They probably don't need to see; the navigation was set and they would only have to remove autopilot when they were approaching their base, whether it is suspended in space or on another planet in a galaxy beyond the gateway. In retrospect, space would make a good prison as escaping and finding your way anywhere in the galaxy would be impossible."

"Maybe we will all end up there," Blaise said.

Savarnee sent a digital laugh in bleeps as we had not incorporated laughing into the digital language we had created. It was all part of our communications with each other – a laugh would denote happiness in a person even if it was at someone else's expense.

We all had different things that made us laugh so we needed the laughs to be incorporated into our language.

We were heading back to Earth now. It seemed we were not living a real life anyway; we were in a surreal place, suspended between two worlds, every time going out there and making new discoveries unparalleled on Earth.

We were pushing the boundaries of our knowledge to another level; it was amazing how far we had come in such a short time. Our brains were so complex in the way we worked and propelled us into other dimensions at colossal speeds unknown to man on Earth, with no spaceship, fuel or oxygen and with no food or drink. How we could even relate to what we were doing seemed impossible and incomprehensible. It was just like a dream you have in a deep sleep and you wake up and realise it was just a dream and nothing was real but you had projected your mind into the abyss of space.

Chapter 25

———◆———

We were now living the dream, but even we had to face reality. We were on the way home and we could only dream until the next mission. At least there did not seem any threat to Earth from a race from another world. We were as safe as we could be at the moment. We were coming back to base and we would hope to be back as soon as we could but we would have to wait our turn to go back. We desperately wanted to go to Mars and have a look around it; there must be some kind of life living there.

There were signs of life on Mars; was there some alien power on there, projecting the square mist clouds? Having the sharp corners, they were so strange but possibly hiding something. Was it the way the atmosphere was formed into square sectional clouds? We still did not know what formed the clouds – was it water vapour or dust or something we had never encountered? We would have to do a full evaluation of the substance that made them.

Everything we did at this moment was secret and we would never inform any authority or dare to tell a soul, as their disbelief in what we told them would be enormous and would create too many questions about what we were doing in the laboratory outside our normal work. The consequences could be dire if they found out.

We would have to keep a tight lid on what we had discovered. We would have to look more at Mars and the strange clouds and what they were covering; also the gateway at the side of it. We needed more clarification of what was going off down there and why spacecraft were disappearing down the gateway. We would all have to agree a strategy as to what to prioritise first; what was going to be our first call into another world? We were somewhere between the devil and the deep blue sea... whatever way we jumped, it would have its own consequences.

Only time would tell if we had made the right decision, but either way, we were on a mission. We all decided on a meeting to see who was going. We needed to make some headway towards creating a weapon. We needed to be in a position to defend ourselves from any potential attackers. We needed to see some major progress on the development of the weapon, but that alone would be groundbreaking work; it would possibly be the most dangerous weapon known to man.

For the present, we would have to tread cautiously so as not to be seen. if we could remain virtually invisible we would not need to defend ourselves. We were going to have to be vigilant in our approach to Mars and the gateway as they could be linked in some way.

We were all excited to see who was going to go, but for now, we were going to be heading off home and meeting in the morning before 10 am.

Adam phoned Amanda for her thoughts on the mission and she said, "I might be going. I think we will all have to throw ourselves into the hat and see what pops out."

"Yeah," Adam said. "I'm good with that; we will have to see how lucky we are. I can't wait until tomorrow."

The night went fast and we were all in the laboratory early. We had placed our names, folded up, in Blaise's baseball cap.

"Ok, let's see how it goes," Amanda said.

Anthony said, "Hey, man, let's go for it. Who wants to pick out three names?"

Blaise leant forward. "I will," he said, shaking up the hat.

Every tag was the same size and colour so it was hard to tell whose each one was. As it was a totally new mission, we had to select the crew this way.

"Savarnee, you pick out the tickets."

Blaise had his hand firmly over the top of the hat so there could be no cheating.

Savarnee put his hand into the hat underneath Blaise's hand and pulled out the first tag. Adam opened it.

"It's me!" he shouted. "I'm going!"

Savarnee went in again, pulled out the next tag and gave it to Adam. He opened it slightly and everybody, at the same time, said, "Come on; get it open."

He looked inside, playing around.

"No time for playing," Amanda said.

Adam said, "Well you will have time – it isn't you; it's Anthony."

"Yeah, man!" Anthony shouted. "I'm going into space."

"Only one ticket left; well, let's do it," Adam said. "Let's see who's coming with the best."

Adam's hand came out really slowly – he was messing about again. He pulled it out and said, "Oh no, it's Amanda,"

Anthony shouted out, "The best team!"

Savarnee said, "No, we are going next so watch this space."

We actually needed Blaise and Savarnee to do our work whilst we were gone and to see if they could make some headway into our new weapon. The three of us were good to go. we had a meeting and decided to explore what was behind the strange, clouded mist hanging over Mars. If we found nothing interesting, short of landing, then we were going to try to explore the gateway next to

Mars. It had a kind of calling to go down there further; it was a spine-chilling place, black and no light. We would have to map our co-ordinates as we travelled into the darkness of it.

Chapter 26

———◆———

While we were away, Blaise and Savarnee would have to make progress on the space mapping we were supposed to be doing for the company. We were off exploring space; we had been shrunk and were ready to move on to the intergalactic adventure onto Mars and to discover the secrets of the gateway. Then, if we found the cloud on Mars to be just odd-shaped cloud cover, we would dart down the gateway.

We were all aware of the danger and would have to keep our presence to a minimum to avoid being discovered by an alien species.

The window was open and we were flying… travelling just shy of the speed of light. We estimated our speed at around 170,000 miles per second. We were virtually invisible – just a trail behind showed something had come through space fast… lightning speed to be more accurate. We were close to Mars; we needed to slow down as we had no means of stopping suddenly.

We had learned to limit speed when we were close to a planet so we didn't pass by, but we were space travellers now and we had to be in control of ourselves and judge the speed to the destination before landing on it. We could see the clouds around the rear of Mars and Adam said,

"Let's go under and see what is there."

Anthony said, "Hey, man, let's go in there quick."

Amanda said, "No, let's proceed with caution. We don't know what the hell is under those clouds and you two want to rush in where fools fear to tread… are you both mad?"

"Well, you have a good point," Adam said.

"Hey, man," Anthony replied.

"Ok, let's go in slow in a straight line to keep our presence to a minimum," Amanda said. "We don't want to be alerting the entire planet to our arrival. Let's keep it down and nice and tight flying in there; no maverick stunts going in, please. Ok, I will take up the helm and go first; you both follow but keep close."

We flew straight under the cloud. We could see the planet's surface.

"Here it is," Adam said. "Nobody else on Earth has ever been here."

There seemed to be a lot of volcanic activity. It didn't seem a stable planet and there were strange square-shaped lakes of lava bubbling. Could this be what was causing the clouds to have square edges? We had done nothing more than glimpse them as we flew by.

There seemed to be defined corners to the lakes as if someone had dug them out to harvest the molten rock. It seemed an inhospitable place to be living. We had all decided that we would take more of a look and explore Mars later. What we really wanted to do was to see what was happening in the gateway.

Could there be life there? Was that why the spaceships were making a beeline for the hole? Was it a connecting tunnel to another galaxy? There had to be more to it. In the vastness of space, was the unknown waiting for us to discover it? What had already been discovered by an alien race? Effectively, we might be only looking for trouble by invading another world. We had not been invited anywhere and we were trespassing with intent. We were a conquering world, violent and cruel, relentless in our conquests; no race more primitive than us would be accepted as an equal.

Domination from Earth would lead to their peril; they would take no prisoners and would enslave everyone on the planet for the benefit of Earth. Maybe we should not explore elsewhere, but first, look at Earth and sort out our own wars and battles before expanding our boundaries into other worlds. The Achilles' heel was that we were militant and an enslaving world, an evolving deadly species, hell-bent on power and greed.

It would be only a matter of time before we had the weapons we could take with us in some form and we would have other intentions than making peace with alien nations. We were a planet steeped in violent history and our armies would soon be on the march into other worlds with the sole intention of stripping the planets of their resources and inhabitants. What kind of people were we?

These missions could lead to the demise of planets unknown; we should not have to worry about UFOs and spaceships coming to Earth – we were the invading source that everybody else should be fearing. We had found a way to travel and we were on our way… hell was on its way, and woe betide any race that got in our pathway.

We were already on the way down the gateway. Adam was digitally mapping the co-ordinates to ensure our return. We could not afford to be lost in space, so it was paramount that a course was mapped – we should never just go somewhere on a whim.

It was pitch black, blacker than coal. There were no stars to lead the way but our take was that the spaceships going down the gateway would have to take the same path as us. It was obviously going to end up somewhere; we had not come all this way for nothing. We were determined to go as far as our connections with our brains would take us. We were making good time; lightning speed was behind us now. We were flying with Adam and Anthony on Amanda's wing.

Adam said, "It should be called moronic speed."

Amanda asked, "Why's that then?"

Adam replied in full digital course, "Only a moron would fly at this speed in the abyss of space." Amanda laughed.

Anthony shouted, "Hey, man, get on it; let's fly."

Amanda was setting the travel speed at the helm.

"Keep your distance from each other, boys; you never know when we might have to make a fast manoeuvre to avoid a collision. We are in total darkness travelling at nearly the speed of light so we need to be aware of any space junk, meteorites or any other things. There are no sun's rays in the gateway – maybe, if we find another galaxy at the bottom of it, there may be light again."

"That would be good," Adam said.

"Hey, man," Anthony replied. He never said too much – 'hey, man' was his opening vocabulary and it was now being recognised intergalactically. Well, at least that was what Anthony thought.

We could all see light in the distance. There was another galaxy at the end of the gateway; that's where all the spacecraft would be going. It was getting lighter the closer we went, so there was definitely a sun for the sunlight it emitted. At last, we came into a vast open space of pure light. There were planets all over the place, very close to each other; some no more than 10 million miles away. This galaxy had a sun and two moons. It was so much brighter than Earth as they were all in a parallel orbit. The planets all seemed to be active in the fact that there was water on a lot of them; some were blue, some turquoise and mixed colours.

Chapter 27

———◆———

We were definitely not alone. We could see lines across space, trails of spaceships crossing galaxies. We were all really excited with what we had found. We transmitted back to Savarnee and Blaise but the signal was weak. They also sent a message to us that if it was a weak signal, we might be at the extent of our brains' capability. This could be possibly as far as we could go. We would have to limit how far we travelled in one go to ensure we did not lose the transmission. We would have to reevaluate what our parameters were and whether we could expand the capabilities of the brain to extend the travel distance and communications. We could not be lost in space without support or unable to communicate back to Earth. How far would a digital signal travel? What limit would there be on a cranial brainwave? Could we also upgrade the brain's potential to project us further into space?

For now, we were at the front of a new galaxy so close to our own; ours appeared dead and lifeless. This new galaxy seemed to be able to sustain multiple life forms on its planets, which were colourful and looked fit for habitation. There was no sign of dying planets – everything was blue and multi-coloured. It was mystical and magical at the same time. We were all in awe of how beautiful it was. We had literally seen other worlds now and they were magnificent in their entirety.

This galaxy was something totally different to what we knew. We didn't know how beautiful a galaxy could be – it was totally awesome; nobody would ever believe what we had seen or comprehend what this place was like. It appeared like an oasis in a desert… something you're desperate to find but can never see. There was so much beauty here never seen from any telescope. We were looking at potentially dead planets in the Milky Way and dreaming there could be life existing there. How could the planets be dead? The whole solar system here was alive. It had a sun and two moons lighting the whole galaxy.

There must have been 30 planets in this galaxy. This is what you would call an immaculate conception. The creator had put a lot of time in here. It was stunning in its appearance yet it was apparently just around the corner from Earth. How could this be so amazing and our galaxy be so boring with its cold grey planets? Our planet system was either old or new; would our solar system evolve into this new galaxy? We would be clueless in our pursuit of the truth to the age of our galaxy and whether Earth was the only young planet.

We couldn't wait to explore this new galaxy. If we could extend our range of travel, then maybe we could find out more about what was happening in other worlds. After all, this was just an oasis lost in the desert of space. Would we be able to reach the end of this galaxy and ones beyond if they existed beyond our imagination? What would still be waiting for us to discover? I'm not sure they would be ready for us. Yet, it seemed their lives were so tranquil with no wars – there seemed to be peace here in this lost world.

We were all excited to be coming back here, however, we would not extend our range as we could all be lost in space. The only powering force was the emitting power of the brains propelling us into the future. We would have to return as we needed to see what we could do to move on into other worlds. The team were all ready to discover everything in this new solar system. We would have unprecedented times ahead of us, but for now, we were on our way back.

Adam and Anthony were counting down the time to when it would be them as a team going it alone into the undiscovered and being able to map out new worlds for us to show our planet what pioneers we all were. This was dangerous talk and could land us all in prison for a long time since we had no mandate to go anywhere into space. We would be stirring up a wasp's nest for someone else to deal with.

If it all went wrong, we could be followed back to Earth and Earth could be invaded by an alien power. We could end up being responsible for World War Three, but this time, it would not be an invading country but an alien species defending its territorial boundaries. They had set their own boundaries well before we knew anything. They would be far in advance of us if they could travel quickly and reach Earth fast. Their technology in weaponry would be immense and we could not be firing our substandard missiles at an invading force as they would be so far advanced they would not even get near them.

We would all have to look again at the liabilities we were creating for mankind on Earth. Why would we continue in our maverick ways, possibly to the detriment of all nations on the planet?

We were near to Earth and our blue planet was equal to any we had encountered on our journey, but it was lost in space in what seemed to be a lifeless galaxy. It seemed everybody had been and gone and we were the remnants of an ancient time long ago. We flew straight in; everything was in place, including Blaise and Savarnee to meet us and find out everything we had discovered.

We had to be more prepared for what we were going to meet on future missions. It would not all be merely observing the new species on the planets; there would have to be some interaction with their worlds. There had been one in the distance with sparkling belts around it like Saturn but on a much bigger scale. You could see it shining out above any other planet. It seemed that the rays coming from the sun were caught in a triangle of sparkling light so bright you could not fix yourself on it – you were mesmerised by its beauty.

Blaise and Savarnee would have to help us draw up a conclusion on what it could have been around the planet to give off so many beautiful blinding rays of light. It was late and we had, as normal, been out longer than we should have been. In future, we needed to focus more on time.

Chapter 28

———◆———

We had overextended our time on the space travel before heading back to Earth. Team leader Amanda was on us straight away not to be too excited and led us into the laboratory. It had been an enlightening experience and everyone was buzzing. It was possible that we had found a galaxy of new friends and would be able to extend the knowledge of our planet. We were due for a meeting about our mission but it would wait until the morning as everyone was too excited thinking about the new galaxy.

Tomorrow would be another day, and we had so much to do to get things back up to speed. We were hyped up so much that we decided to go for a meal and talk over tomorrow's strategies. Then we could come in fresh with the right attitude to move on and fix all the problems we were incurring and to be able to progress further into other worlds.

Morning was here and we sat around the laboratory clearing up our usual work and then talking about how work was progressing on the weapons we were trying to make to defend us. Blaise and Savarnee had been making new inroads into the innovative lasers. It would not be possible to take them into space but, with accurate co-ordinates, they would be able to destroy spaceships and alien species.

They were in the final stages of a tracker laser that would track and destroy invading forces. They had managed to get the laser ray to leave the laboratory, break its connection from the laser and travel to the target at beyond lightning speed, instantly vaporising the target. It was probably the deadliest weapon on the planet. We were so far ahead of the military all over the world as we could destroy any target anywhere, here or in space. We were doing so much to make the world an even more dangerous place than what it is now. We were instrumental in opening up potential world wars. We would have to tread more carefully in our approach to weaponry.

We would be in the lab most of the day. There would be no more missions today until we could try to extend the range of the brain's communication – definitely a difficult problem. At least we had some defence now with the laser; it just needed a trial run. However, as yet, we had nobody that created a risk to us so it would be on the back burner waiting for the right time.

We were all hoping we would never have to use it; we were more focused on getting the team out there to discover the new galaxy. There would be lots to discover; our concern was how welcome we would be. We had no idea – how welcome would we be to an alien landing on Earth? We were going to be on our way soon and we were all excited at our new discovery.

It was the turn of Savarnee and Blaise but Adam would be heading it as team leader. We would be off in minutes and we were ready to go. We launched ourselves out the window, off to another world; it sent shivers down our spines. We all felt it, although only from our minds as we were just atoms fired into space. However, we were definitely three entities flying through space, discovering new worlds and being able to fully communicate and see everything as it happened. We were hoping it was going to be a successful mission but only the end of our trip would tell us the results.

We were rounding Mars towards the gateway and Adam said,

"Ok, boys, can you close up? We need to keep it tight as we don't want to be lost here. We have the co-ordinates but we also have to be vigilant to alien spacecraft that might pick us up on their communications equipment.

We don't want to be discovered so let's keep it tight and hold off on conversations unless urgent."

"Ok, team leader," Blaise and Savarnee replied.

"Let's go; follow my lead," Adam said. Adam had named the gateway Paradise Way as he was convinced it led to a paradise of planets with nice people on them.

He was someone who took people at face value instead of getting to know them first. It would be a dangerous mistake to make, especially where we were going, and it would be enlightening, to say the least. We had turned and entered the gateway; we had cut back on speed due to the darkness. It seemed to be a long time waiting to see the light at the end of the tunnel. We were coming towards open space and we could see all the planets.

"Wow! Look at this!" Savarnee said.

"Yeah," Blaise replied, "that's definitely something I have never ever seen in my wildest dreams! It's awesome... unbelievable."

"I can't wait to see it all," Adam said. "Let's go and proceed with caution as we are strangers here and we don't want any alien force knowing we are here. Keep it together; we are going in."

We were approaching the first planet. Something was different, Adam said, but he couldn't quite put his finger on what it was. Yet it had his sensors on overdrive.

"Let's take it steady; there is something not right here. I can feel the sensors are playing havoc with my mind and the brain is picking up on something. Let's not be too…"

"Wow!" Savarnee said, Adam being cut short on his chat. There they were two small spacecraft right above us – they seemed to have come from nowhere.

"Let's try and lose them before they see us," Adam said.

"Ok, team leader," Blaise replied. "Yes, I am definitely going with that. Let's stay on course and head towards the glittering planet. I'm sure they can sense us… something is opening on the underside of the spaceship. It does not look friendly; it looks like a laser."

"Yes, I can see it too," Savarnee said.

"Pull back!" Blaise said. "I think they are going to fire! Let's get out of here. I think we can outrun them if we try."

As quick as the laser door opened, it closed as we passed underneath. Was it some kind of sensor or ventilation door, or even a garbage hatch? We were flying underneath them and we agreed we had probably not been detected. We carried on past the first two planets. Moving out, forward or back could lead to us being seen and we didn't need that. The two craft were strange in their construction – almost like an arrow, with the helm in the tip of the space-craft, with a large rear passenger or cargo hold, similar to our planes but with a rear dart-like tail. There seemed to be an engine in the front and one directly in the same position at the back. Strange to have an engine in the front unless it was on a propulsion system, horizontally pulling the spaceship along and the rear pushing it.

Chapter 29

———◆———

They were travelling at high speed. We had to keep up with them until they changed course; that way, we could drop away as they turned and we could be on their blind side. Whoever they were, they were far more advanced than us. They could do space travel with matter where it would be hundreds of years before we were at their level of technology. We were concerned we would run out of distance for our signals and not be able to come back to Earth. We were not in a good place at the moment. All of a sudden, Adam sent a message:

"Get ready – we're in trouble. I can see three spacecraft right in front of us and these don't look like the others. They have definitely been sent to blow us out of space; they're arming the weapons, I can see the door opening. Dive!"

As we dived, you could see the line of the laser as they fired.

"Wow! That was lucky!" Adam said. "Let's go lightning speed and try and outrun them."

Now, we could see the two craft we were following had let their command centre know our position and sent their fighter craft to take us out. This was not the sign of a friendly alien; they would be vicious in every way if they could. They just fired without hesitation. They didn't even want to know us; all they wanted to do was destroy us, so it wasn't the idyllic galaxy we thought. These had real spacecraft and a real defence strategy; they were not going to welcome anybody here.

They were closed for business; no one was coming into their domain.

They were behind us, still running us out of their galaxy and back to the gateway we had come down. They were relentless in their pursuit, firing at us, the lasers coming above and below us as they fired. We were on the run, fleeing for our atom lives. We were not sure whether if we were terminated as atoms our brains would die as well. We had manoeuvred our way out of the lasers; just as well, since one blast of laser was enough to vaporise us all.

We could see the distance it went before fizzling out… one on target would totally annihilate us.

We were at top speed just outrunning them, but we were putting distance between us. We were definitely more advanced in speed but we had no idea what they could have that was faster than us. We could see the lasers coming past us, so we knew we had got them lagging behind us. Finally, they were no longer reaching us as we had outrun them.

We were on our way out through the gateway, still at top speed; we would not be hanging about. We needed to get out fast as there could be other spacecraft waiting for us at the other end. We had no idea where their boundaries finished; we could only assume it was here but where had the first spacecraft we saw disappearing down the gateway come from – out of our galaxy? Would they end up beyond the new galaxy into other gateways?

For now, we were glad to be on our own in this one. We shot out the gateway faster than a laser beam.

Adam said, "All clear; let's go home."

"I never thought we would get out of that. If only we could have used our own laser, we could have ended it without the chase," Blaise said, "but we could have had World War Three on our doorstep in the morning. How would we be able to fight aliens with the technology they have? We could never win the war; they would totally destroy our planet. We need to possibly go a different way home rather than directly because we don't want to leave a trail for them to follow."

There was only one laser capable of firing that far into space and it was ours. We could not let on to anybody that we had been making a weapon… trouble would surely follow. Although the government would appreciate the technology, they might reward us in the way of a long prison sentence. We tried to zigzag our way back but, whatever way we went, I'm sure they would find us. Had we opened up a wasp's nest going into their galaxy?

It seemed nothing was going to be the same again. It seemed now only a matter of time before they came to give us a bloody nose for sticking it into their business. We were not wanted there and they had made that more than clear by trying to obliterate us. The only way was to be able to outrun them but that would be futile if they sprang a surprise attack on us. We might have to leave more space between us so, at least if one of us was taken out by them, they would not take out the whole team at once.

We would have to be vigilant in future missions.

Blaise said, "Yeah, after today, I might stay at base; it's safer ."

Savarnee replied, "You only live once; let's do it."

Adam said, "We nearly did do it for good ."

Everyone was agreed we should talk out all the new strategies we needed to conform to. To make it all work, we couldn't come back here until we had a plan. For now, it had opened our eyes to the danger of just cruising through space like we owned it.

We were in the unknown and we got a taste of it today. We were glad to be back and safe. Amanda and Anthony said they weren't quite as excited as they had been about going into space, but was there any more risk than being shrunk to an atom?

Adam said, "Yes, but that is tried and tested."

We needed more clarification before we could make a decision to stay or continue to travel into space with all the risks it encompassed. We were going to have some time just to see what happened. We took a vote and everyone voted to go regardless of risks. We all wanted to be pioneers of space – nobody was quitting for one setback. We were going for it.

Chapter 30

———◆———

If they wanted trouble, we had a weapon so we could fight back. We were a planet of conquerors, not a feeble race of cowards. We were going to give as much as we got – space belonged to everybody, not just one race to control it all. We were going in the morning as usual – there would be no breaks in our routine. The human race was on the march and look out to whoever got in our way. We would have to see who the third person would be in the team – it might be better in twos to reduce our risk and the chance of being seen. Two, one behind the other, would be harder to see but not having a wing buddy did put a certain amount of risk on it all. Regardless, we were going. Amanda was going with Anthony and we would see how the mission went with only two people.

As space pilots, they were both ready for the mission. Nothing would stop us now – we were even more determined to go and were excited to be leaving. We had gone through so much just to give it all away. We were the

21st-century explorers and we were about to put some space between Earth and us.

We had left a sonic boom as we cleared the clouds. We were travelling at lightning speed – a flash of light was all anybody on Earth could see as we launched into space. We weren't even sure if anybody would even know what or who we were; all that mattered was that we were left to discover the undiscovered.

We were making good time. It seemed the more journeys we made, the faster we seemed to get there. We had tweaked the power from the brains to allow better communication between the base and the atoms. It seemed like the upgrade was giving slightly more speed and we were flying. It was so good to be going on a mission. Would we be in the firing line? We wouldn't know but we were hell-bent on seeing this galaxy and no alien power was going to dissuade us, even if we were 1000 years too early.

We would never be able to get there in a spacecraft for years to come. We were the present and we were here sooner than they probably thought. We had rounded Mars and could see the gateway in the distance. It looked deserted; no sign of life in the distance. We reduced our rate from lightning speed to billispeed, just really ticking over, and the brains were having a rest as we cruised into the abyss of space. All seemed good – we could not see or hear any activity. Everything was quiet… maybe they thought they had seen the back of us on the chase out the gateway.

We were further into the galaxy than the other team had gone and we had not been detected by any alien force. It must be due more to luck than judgement. We had our eyes and ears peeled for the slightest noise or sight of any spacecraft. There seemed there were none in the vicinity. Most of the spacecraft must possibly be powered by a kind of atomic propulsion of some description. Evolution in this galaxy would have taken them beyond nuclear power – possibly fusion or magnetic energy where there were no emissions into space. Space here was clean; there was no space junk like our galaxy. We had been off-loading junk satellites and rockets into space for years.

The first planet looked so colourful with lots of blues and greens; not as bright as the others, and it seemed the furthest away from the sun, which was the brightest of the galaxy. It was tremendous in its format. Here, you would be able to see all the planets in the galaxy from a telescope without any infrared lights. Everything seemed light although it was day. Possibly it would be as black as the gateway we came down at night. We would be exploring the first planet; there was no sense in passing other planets because one was shining out more than the others. Going further would not be good as we would not be aware of what might be behind us blocking our escape.

It would be our first planet in our new galaxy. Discovering a universe would be another task too much. There were possibly hundreds of galaxies; even as many as a million… space was endless. How could anything be so enormous? It was something unimaginable. We had to take it step by step, and the first was to discover the planet in front of us. We would name it Intro after the word 'introduction'; all we had to do was discover what was living on it.

Chapter 31

The planet was so colourful there would have to be life on it. We got to the outer limits surrounding it. We would have to break through the atmosphere to be able to scout the planet in its entirety. We could not see any movement but there were lots of domed-style mounds with wire crisscrossing the tops in a square fashion yet perfect in its design. Were these for storage? They were igloo-style in shape. The landscape seemed to be overgrown with trees and large mountainous areas with dark blue lakes and sandy shores around the lakes. They appeared to probably be as deep as the oceans as the mountains were high, indications of life with the trees and the blue water.

The clouds over the land were classic signs that there would be fresh water and life on the planet but we spotted no one as we flew by. The planet seemed deserted; nothing happening but these strange dome-shaped buildings. We would have to land and have a look at the domes to see what they were and why there was no life here. The planet could sustain life… or could it be that there could be poisonous gases here that had probably stopped life existing? It looked so much like Earth; it was inviting and there could not be a good reason for people not being here. Would it be a place to colonise for earthlings?

We were going to have to land and try and mimic whatever race we could find that we could look like. If it was a dead planet, we would stay as atoms and try to infiltrate the dome structures to find out if there was life on this planet. Amanda decided, as she was the team leader, that she should go in first to the dome if there was enough room to fly in without putting us in danger. As we had never crashed, we were not sure how we would survive the experience. Anthony was going to follow me in but we would have to scout to see if there would be another way out in case we were trapped inside.

"Ok, Anthony, let's go for it," Amanda said.

"Ok, team leader. I'm with you."

"Keep right behind me, Anthony."

"Hey, man, I'm here."

We went straight through a flap that was open.

"It's massive in here, Anthony. Be careful. We will have to land and hide somewhere; we can't be incarcerated on this planet. There doesn't seem to be any life here."

We decided to park up on top of a shelf in the structure just to see if there was anything moving in the dome.

There was a basement-type area, typical of a chamber in the Colosseum in Rome where they kept all the gladiators and animals to go into the arena. There was something not quite right – we could hear a noise outside the dome which sounded like a hum from a machine. Something had landed and we saw human-looking aliens being driven into the domes.

Their faces were expressionless and they only had one finger and a thumb to each hand. The way they walked was almost like a primitive man. Their hair was in a bun on the top of their heads; it looked as if no one had ever had their hair cut.

Apart from being white with no hair on their bodies, they looked prehistoric. They were shuffling in and making a strange type of squeaking, more like a shrilled piercing sound. They were being herded like cattle, huddling in a circle as they entered the dome, their heads looking to the floor with their arms over their heads covering them as much as they could. The door closed behind them. The moonlight shone through the steel banding over the dome making it twinkle inside, bouncing back off the side wires.

Why had they been brought here and left? We were trying to guess. Then we saw hundreds of spider-like insects, around the height of the aliens, spilling into what we now knew as an arena. The humanoids had been brought in purposely as food. The spiders looked vicious as they ran into the dome from under the ground. They had a large human head but a spider's body and teeth like a shark. You could see them with their mouths open, running into the arena, bloodthirsty, wanting to feed on the humanoids. They were just food, like mice for a cat. They pinned the humanoids to the ground, but the humanoids were trying to keep their hands on their heads as if they knew what was coming. Were these intelligent humanoids or virtually prehistoric in their brains?

They were all doing the same thing, so obviously, they knew they had to survive the spider attack. All the spiders were surrounding the humanoids when a shrill siren went off. It was obviously the signal that dinner was served as they literally jumped on top of the humanoids and started to eat, with the spiders and their shark-like teeth making their way down through the hands to the head.

There were shrilling noises everywhere as the spiders feasted on them. They seemed to enjoy chewing bits out of the head whilst holding them down with their four legs. They were not like our eight-legged ones; these had evolved as pure killing machines, killing in a gruesome way by chewing all the heads off.

Every spider did exactly the same as the bodies fell to the ground. Whilst they were still moving, probably just the nerves making the bodies twitch, they started cocooning the bodies and they left the silk hanging out of their abdomen to drag it away. They all started to drag the humanoids, or what was left of them, into the underground lair.

The way they died was barbaric and macabre. Where were they getting the humanoids from and what was the purpose of the spiders being there? It didn't make any sense why they should bring them to the pods for the spiders to kill and eat them. We understood it was keeping the spiders alive, but for what purpose? Were the spiders prisoners too, and if so, who had dropped them off here? Where had they come from?

Other insects, which looked a bit like giant cockroaches, had come out of the basement and were cleaning up what the spiders had left. One was charging out of the arena with an eyeball in its mouth. They had enormous strength and could carry five times their own weight. Their look was somewhere between a donkey and a cockroach, with the legs of a donkey and the head of an ant but the hard back of a cockroach. They ran so fast to get the food away from the others; it looked like it was dog-eat-dog out there.

The fastest one won the prize… hardly a prize but food – to an insect needing nourishment, it was a life-saver.

We had seen enough here; the brutal attack on the human-oids had made sense. Although barbaric, it had brought it home that this world had to survive like the next. How they killed or harvested food was not our concern at this time.

We would have to get back as it was getting late; this was only the beginning of a new chapter in our missions to other galaxies. What we were now concerned about was how we would get out of the galaxy back to Earth. We had been lucky coming in not to be discovered, so we would have to be alert on the way out. It was not a good experience. Our thoughts that it would be a dream place to visit and find nice approachable aliens turned out to be incorrect. What we had seen was a massacre of alien beings eaten by spider-type insects bigger than a human, human-oids being brought in for food to feed savage insects.

There would be no reason for this unless the spiders were the masters of the planet and food was being brought to their domain. The only reason we could come to was that they had evolved more than our spiders into fearsome insects, stronger than two tigers together. These were not something you could ever let loose as they would destroy everybody on a planet. I predicted that is exactly what they had done. We started to make our way off the planet; we were out of time.

Chapter 32

————◆————

We were approaching Mars; we had come all this way back with no sign of any spacecraft. We had the whole of space to ourselves and we were on a clear way back to base. We had radioed in and everything was good there and they were expecting us back as normal. As we were passing Mars, we could see Earth. The sun was setting in front, so as the Earth was turning, it was our turn to be in the darkest of space with the Earth blocking out the sun's rays as we made our way there. Home lay just in front of us when we saw tracer lasers coming at us from Mars on the Earth side of the planet.

There must have been a base or a spacecraft on the planet as they could sense us coming by them. They were accurate as we were having to manoeuvre.

"Dive!" Amanda said. "Let's go deep out of their range."

Anthony said, "Hey, man, let's go for it ."

We both got into a bottomless dive. We had no idea where we would end up but space was endless… there was no top or bottom… just unlimited darkness of nothing but space. We had dived as fast and as far as we could. We were still in reach of transmission but no laser was going to be useful here.

We had messaged back to tell them at base. Were they waiting for us or was it just coincidence? Could it have been a trap to laser us out of space into a burning light before we fizzled out like a firework? We were lucky this time – we had not been looking and we were caught napping as we passed Mars. We would not make the same mistake twice. We would have to tell the others to be aware of what was lurking in deep space… under us, over us, behind a planet… anywhere we could be ambushed by an alien force.

They were out there and space was no longer a friendly place to be. There would be peril if we merely threw caution to the wind. We could not afford to pay no attention to where we were going and what was out there waiting in the wings to take us out. We had travelled well beyond Earth on the underside of our planet to get away from who was firing the ray and to take the scent off our destination. We did not want them to know our origin planet, so Earth had only sent missions out to close areas like the moon, Mars and Saturn. These were mostly unmanned missions as technology was not so far advanced in the field of space exploration. Only the team knew about our missions.

We arrived back late; the team had waited for us to come back to base. Anthony and Amanda flew in around 8 pm; it had been a long time for them. Their brains must have also been exhausted; they would have to rest although not for long. They had a way of sustaining long spells of space travel; besides, they would rest as they would not be going on tomorrow's mission.

Amanda said, "I would like to go if anyone pulls out, I will volunteer."

"Fat chance of that," Adam said. "We are going where you have been; it sounds like a ball."

"Ha!" Amanda said. "You weren't there! It was grue-some; I couldn't believe what happened to those poor souls and the way they all died. It's like they knew exactly what was coming… there was some form of intelligence there."

We had told the team what to expect and they would remain aware of the alien forces that were in the new galaxy. We had also told them that they were enslavers of humanoids and harvesters of humanoids for food for giant spiders and that they incarcerated the spiders in gladia-tor-style domes. Adam and Blaise would have to be vigi-lant as whoever they were that brought the humanoids would not be taking any prisoners.

They would have to keep their eyes peeled for the unexpected. We could not afford any of the team to be killed or captured as we didn't think we would be seeing them back. They would not be treated well.

The team had now extended their reach into the galaxy, but we had to see what was beyond the first planet, Intro. Amanda and Anthony said it was deserted except for the domes and the spiders that lived in them. Adam and Blaise might be able to scout the planet to see if there were any other signs of life we may have missed, although there were no signs of habitation – no structures to show anybody living there, but the planet was suitable for human life to exist on.

As Adam and Blaise were on the way there, Adam messaged:

"We are approaching Mars so we are on the way to the gateway. I will go the opposite way around Mars to avoid any future ambush that could be waiting for us and to see if there are any signs of aliens parked up in a spacecraft waiting for our revisit." Blaise called in to base: "No signs of any activity here."

"Ok, Blaise," Amanda replied.

All was good – so far, we were having a good run. We would be meeting the planet Intro soon, so we would be on the lookout for any spacecraft, there would be no ambush this time. We were fully aware of their presence and we had speed on our side, or so it appeared.

This was due to our size and power emitted from the brain pulse. We were travelling at lightning speed and beyond. We arrived at Intro and scouted the whole planet, including the oceans; there seemed to be no life there. What was here? Nothing really, it was waiting for evolution to advance. We needed to bring life from Earth and install animals and sea creatures here to see if we could accelerate the evolution process by five million years. The plant life was here but there were no animals or birds to colonise the planet. All the food was here to sustain life but nothing seemed to have been cultivated.

It was wild… mainly all forest. Maybe there could be life living amongst the trees or under the sea. We would not be spending any more time around this planet, however, we were hoping there would be colonies on the other planets we were visiting. The galaxy was too bright and the planets too colourful not to be habitable by life forms unknown to us.

"Let's go," Blaise said. "We need to go to the next one."

We made a fast run and orbited around the planet; it had rings around it. Adam said,

"Let's call it 'Sphere' as it sounds like a good name to call a planet."

"Yeah," Blaise said. "That's a good name; let's do it. That's two planets named."

We rounded the planet. This one definitely had life on it as we could see air traffic moving around the cities. This was it – we would be making new friends here.

"I'm sure they are friendly," Blaise said. "It looks busy down there."

In seconds, there were spacecraft all around us with blacked-out windows. We could not see their faces but we saw that something was moving around in the cockpit. Still, we could not work out what or who they were. They were in virtual darkness, but there were lights flashing on all the spacecraft. They wanted to escort us in, but this was not how we wanted to discover their planet. They were highly evolved; possibly 500 years ahead of us, but we had discovered what a human brain can do.

They probably did not have the same mental ability as us; we had evolved well as a species. We were now going to be prisoners, not guests, and this was not going to end well. They had us escorted towards the planet we had named Sphere. There was going to have to be a plan and we would have to hope they had not discovered our digital language. Blaise was talking about going down to the planet's surface and escaping.

"There would be no escaping from there," Adam said. "We have to do something fast; there will be a short time as they re-enter the atmosphere when we might be able to get away as the compressing gases would cause the nose cones of the spacecraft to heat up. They will not be able to manoeuvre into the planet's atmosphere just for the 100 seconds going through, so we could make a run for it."

"Ok, got that," Blaise said.

"Right," Adam said, "follow me; let's try and get under the rear, not too far away or they will not enter the atmosphere. When I say, break to the right and let's dive, turn into a vertical thrust and let's get out of here as they enter the atmosphere. The gases will compress and they need to have the heat shields active to absorb the compressing gases or they will burn up on re-entry. As they are going through re-entry, we will be gone. They will have to turn and virtually take off again. We don't have to do any of that due to our size and composition as we will not displace the gases at the same rate so we don't suffer burn-up as we re-enter. Break!"

We both broke to the right and went vertical at lightning speed back into space.

"Wow! Yeah!" Blaise shouted as we rocketed into outer space.

Chapter 33

————◆————

There would be no one following that manoeuvre – it was something else. They would have never seen that one coming. There was no sign of any spaceships; we had outsmarted them and they would never catch us now. We were long gone. about to enter the gateway. Intro was behind us and Mars in front. At least we had discovered Sphere, the second planet in the new galaxy. We needed a name for our new discovery; we would have to make a group decision on it all. Amanda transmitted a message:

"Have a safe journey back, boys, we will see you soon ."

We could see Earth – it seemed safe looking at it but, wherever there were people, there were wars going off and people killing others for no particular reason but greed for control or money.

As we approached it, you would believe we were looking after it… far from the truth. It was a time bomb waiting to go off, with some foreign power wanting to seize other nations' territory or assets. There would always be war here. With our violent intentions between each race and creed, one day, this planet may cease to exist. Would we ever find peace anywhere in any galaxy where there would be an equilibrium where people or beings could live in harmony? Was I just sounding off?

"Yes," Blaise said, as we flew through the window into the laboratory.

"Welcome back, boys," Amanda said.

"Hey, man," Anthony also blurted out.

"Welcome back, men," Savarnee said. "It looks like you two have been having fun. I could hear lots of action on the transmissions. We thought you were goners; it was a good plan, Adam, to catch them on burn-up at atmosphere level. I bet they never saw you go. It's a good job they were all escorting you and none were in space when you left Sphere. That's a good plan for any other alien races that try to incarcerate us."

We would have to be a step above the competition if we were going to survive space and all it encompassed. It was an uncharted place full of mystery and imagination but fraught with the unknown and the uncertainty of what to expect in this vastness that we were travelling in. It seemed that there was danger everywhere, so we would have to be more vigilant in our missions.

We were determined to keep exploring the new galaxy, and we had decided between us all that Unimars would be an apt name for it as it was hiding just behind Mars. We were all behind it; simple in its name but everybody would know its location. It would be the best name for it.

We were on our way again into space and the unknown. We would soon know who was inhabiting the planet Sphere and if they were friendly or not. We would have to tread cautiously to ensure we were not caught. We would never be able to escape again – all their military would be aware if we were in the vicinity and they would know exactly what they were looking for. We would not be so lucky next time. We were now back in the Unimars, the gateway and getting towards Intro, passing it on the way to Sphere.

When we arrived, Sphere looked busy below and we could see life going on around the planet. It looked like it had really large buildings with monorail-type bars and trains going between each building. Most of the buildings were generally taller and bigger than the average 50-floor skyscraper on Earth. Why did they build these industrial-looking buildings so big? What could possibly be stored in them? We would have to take a look in one of them if we could get in unnoticed. We were just atoms yet we were visible in space. It was probably due to the speed vapour trails as we cut through space. It was like an electric discharge from the lightning speed we were travelling at but we would be going into the industrial units at landing speed only.

We also had to find a space big enough for us to get into but, more importantly, to be able to fly out fast in the event we were seen. We managed to get through an open vent and perched on the beams in the roof of the unit. We were shocked – the whole place was kitted out for warfare. There were robots building spaceships; they were not like we would imagine them to be. They were not using any form of platforms or steps; everything was being done at a form of unimaginable speed. They had propulsion jets all around them, built in so they could move anywhere at breakneck speed. Their system was perfect; they had nearly completed the structure of one in less than one hour. We had never seen anything like it.

If this was the future of building… We were so far behind these robots but we could see no alien beings over-seeing the work being done. The speed of construction was not to be believed; they were programmed to produce hundreds a day but why would they need so many? We tried to get a closer look, but as we moved above the front of the line, Blaise missed the beam and knocked into a metal side panel and it made a noise. There was a robotic eye that moved into the area; it was looking everywhere, shining a laser light, trying to pick up some signs of movement or sight. We were lucky we were on the back of the shelf as it scanned the area.

It was one of those times when, if we had been in our human bodies, we would have been sweating. We could still feel an emotion that was different than we felt when we were in danger; it was a warning signal transmitted to us as the brain picked up on our emotions. The robot eye seemed to be satisfied there was nothing there and went back to its docking station, looking in all directions. As it made its way back to dock, Blaise sent a message:

"Sorry, Adam, just a bit rusty there."

Adam said, "You nearly got us caught. I'm sure that ventilator we flew in an hour ago would not be a way out. If we're discovered, this will have been a big mistake, so you will have to be careful. Let's have a look at the front of the aircraft so we will recognise them if we meet them in space."

There were robots putting a steel webbing all over the front of the spaceships and on the rear engine. These had the long bodies on them; these were definitely what we had first seen as we came into Unimars the first time. They were obviously providing some kind of heat shield in the form of a tight netting and making sure it was on every exposed area. They possibly had the same problems on re-entry to the planet.

Blaise said, "It doesn't look like steel – it's shining differently and not catching the light the same way. It's more like silk."

"That's it," Adam said. "That's why Intro has spiders on it… they're harvesting the silk from the spiders to use as shields. The silk here must have some form of heat resistance to it to enable them to re-enter the atmosphere at speed. It could be that the silk webbing was better than the heat tiles used on rockets and the space shuttle."

They had obviously sorted a source of supply for the silk and they were feeding the spiders and milking them for their silk to use on their spaceships. But why were they in production of so many spacecraft, and why were they building them as fast as cars?

Chapter 34

———◆———

There had to be a reason why there were programmers for the robots building the spaceships. They would need some directions; they could not do it without programming. However, they were just on a production line, doing what robots do in factories on Earth. This was not something new – we had been doing it for years, having robots in factories working day and night. Yet these were different – they were not fixed to anything, just programmed to work wherever they were as if they were wireless.

There was no need for scaffolding, ladders or wired connections. They could also work together lifting big panels into place. They could work in synchronicity with each other, yet they were programmed to think for themselves. The work they did looked flawless. It seemed it was all going together perfectly but at an unbelievable speed. They must have been synchronised together with a Bluetooth-like connection. They were working too perfectly together; they would have to be connected in some way to enable them to keep the pace they were working at.

They would be making the equivalent of hundreds of spaceships per week. Why would they need this amount? It was puzzling why the place appeared to be a factory of motor parts producing spaceships with robots building them on their own. We had to scout and have a look around the cities to see what there was. Would there be someone there we could communicate with?

Blaise said to Adam, "Well, not sure until we get there; let's go and look to see what we can discover here and try to at least make friends."

We flew out easily as the vent had been left open; there was no life here, just robots doing work. There had to be a place where we could communicate with an alien species.

We kept above the clouds where we could see below but could be obscured to others. We didn't want to alert aliens to our presence. We only had two hours before we were out of time so it was going to be a quick fly-over and then back to base. There were space cars and transporters everywhere but there were no roads. Everything moving was in the air and looked built for purpose.

There was nobody walking around. The ground area was deserted but the air was busy with small craft moving about, all on the way to somewhere, darting around each other. We would have to return here on our next visit – it was a place where it seemed everyone was working, doing something for the benefit of the planet. The vehicles in the air had something like an autopilot as they were darting in front of each other at speed. They would have to be like racing drivers to be able to focus properly without crashing as it was a metropolis of crossroads. We could see docking stations; there were no car parks – merely rods sticking out from the buildings where they docked with the front of the vehicle onto the docking pole.

You could see them docked on the platforms to the building for entry. This planet was like New York and London together with the traffic moving around it. There were no traffic lights, stop signs or give ways… they were like dodgem cars, just missing each other as they went by. What else did they make in this city besides spaceships? We were curious to know and we were just guessing at the moment, but these aliens, whoever they were, had everything running to perfection. There had to be something more to this – it was too well organised and regimental in its format.

The team at base were excited we had found this planet with life on it and they were gearing up to take our places the next day. As we moved into the outer atmosphere, we could see spaceships docked around a space station. This was not anything like the space station we shared… this was the size of a large city. We could see spaceships going in and out. They looked the same as the ones in the factory below. Were they a manufacturer of spacecraft to sell to other worlds? Was this the reason they needed so many?

Adam said to Blaise, "I would love to have a look in there."

Blaise said, "You first. I'm not too keen to go in there. I am not sure you would escape from there if they caught you spying on them. They must be well advanced to be able to assemble a monster like this and for it to be a stable base for spacecraft to use."

They were at another level to Earth. If their technology was as good in weaponry as it was in building space stations and spacecraft, we would be no match if they decided to come to Earth.

We would have to have the weaponry to fight off invaders from space. We had come so far but not far enough to protect ourselves against a force like this one, yet it was only a galaxy away. We ran out of time and we were on our way home but it had been enlightening. Blaise said it was "almost scary". We had never seen anything like this before. They looked a dangerous adversary to have looking at you. Everybody at base was getting concerned about what we were doing and whether we were opening a can of worms.

This was an unprecedented moment exploring a world of superior beings. Could we survive an attack if they turned out to be enemies? It would be a team decision on where we would go from here. Were we going to places where we were not welcome? We had at least got back to Earth safely and were now in a dilemma as to what to do. It would be risky going back to the planet again.

Chapter 35

———•———

Savarnee and Anthony were going to be next. They would have to be careful, but at least they now knew what to expect. We needed to know more about what was happening on this planet and all the others in the galaxy. The spacecraft we saw which escorted us into the outer edge of space on their planet were the same spaceships we saw the robots building. They were so fast in their assembly of the spaceships but these were not fixed machines. They were programmed to access all areas of the spaceship – each robot was effectively its own man, you might say. It could do any job on the spaceship but they were programmed to work efficiently together.

There were no breaks or stoppages – it looked a 24-hour-a-day operation.

There was a major build taking place but we as a team could not understand why and where the parts were being made for the assembly of the spaceships. What industry was working in the galaxy? The first planet, Intro, was sparse and overgrown – they were producing only one product... the silk from the spiders. So, were the other planets where the aliens would be working with the robots to produce the parts for the spaceship assembly? We needed to find this out to discover what the aliens were thinking. These were large craft and built to carry loads or military personnel. The production line was enormous but it was just an assembly line – no manufacture was carried out here. We had never seen robots working so fast. It was mind-blowing to watch them work, but we had not encountered any alien forces that were programming the robots to carry out the assembly of spacecraft. Maybe they were on the planet with the gold platinum and silver-looking rings around it. We had to discover why they were building such a large quantity of spaceships and we could probably find out the reason if we could find the masters of the robots.

However, we had more to discover about this galaxy. We were only just on the tip of the iceberg. There was so much more beyond what we had seen already. We were all talking about the planet with the rings around it. We were curious as to what was going off behind the screen of the glittering rings that encircled the planet. Were they rings of dust or was it something that had evolved during the formation of the planetary galaxy?

It would be purely guessing at this time. Adam and Savarnee's thoughts were that the planet might have a magnetic force that was drawing particulates of metal in space towards the planet, causing a whirlpool around it in an orbit of cascading glittering light of different metals, all finding their way into their own orbit and creating a shower of light like a display of a Catherine wheel, a firework spinning in a controllable format held in situ by a magnetic force. We had to be able to find a way through the bands of glitter and onto the surface of the planet to find out if this was the premier planet in the new galaxy.

We were all excited to explore the magnetic planet, but maybe it was uninhabitable due to possible radiation emitted by a magnetic force from the centre of the planet. This was all guesswork as we were not aware what the planet's secrets were. We were all talking about it and Adam and Savarnee were desperate to discover what was on it. We seemed to be like flies flying from one piece of sugar to the next. We needed to slow down our pursuit of finding new species on another planet. We had confirmed there was life beyond our planet and galaxy and we were too curious as to what else we would find on our travels. It was all there, just waiting to be discovered, and we were pioneers of space. No frontier would be an obstacle again.

We would be able to infiltrate any planet. We had the ability to mimic aliens if we needed to fit into any situation.

We had only encountered the humanoids that had been brought to the planet Intro as food for the spiders who produced the heatproof webbing that was being used on the spacecraft. We had yet to discover what was on the new planet.

We were about to visit; we had all decided to call it Sparkle due to the glittering rings that surrounded it. As Anthony "hey man" was busy on the laser weapon, he had the most knowledge on the final parts being added to our shrinking laser. He was forfeiting his turn to work at base on developing the weapon since it was getting near to completion. It was almost ready to test out, but what could we use near Mars to test it on?

We would have to pick out a spot on the surface and see if the laser would hit the spot. Amanda and Savarnee could message us on the way back around Mars on the way home after the voyage to Sparkle. They could wait at Mars, pick out a defined position and see if the laser would do its job and hit the spot. If it was successful, we would have a useable weapon to attack or defend Earth from any alien force sent against us to destroy our way of life. We would have to wait until they were rounding Mars to take them out as we needed a straight line of fire. If he finished it, Anthony could operate the laser with Adam, and Blaise could sort out the co-ordinates. Everybody was multi-tasking but had their own set of skills they encompassed along with a drive to be pioneers of space.

Chapter 36

———— ◆ ————

Amanda and Savarnee had come in early with Adam. They were virtually ready to go by the time Blaise and Anthony arrived. Amanda had been the driving force for an early start to exit the window into space, so she had been ready all night, waiting for the dawn so she could make an early start. Savarnee had arrived not long behind her; he was singing some song from David Bowie's Space Odyssey about some astronaut having trouble in space. Providing the brain kept us travelling, we wouldn't break down; it would be a smooth ride to Sparkle.

The team had all arrived and Blaise would be helping Anthony out on the installation of the laser's modifications. We would be going to another planet and also testing the new weapon out on its performance of range, accuracy and power. It had to do all three in one or it would not be viable as a weapon. We would also have the most powerful weapon in the world and it would possibly rival anything else in the galaxy. We could not predict what weaponry the alien robot-controllers had on their spaceships. They were living a totally different life to us; robots seemed to be creating everything there.

The aliens in charge had also already been quite aggressive to us on our discovery of the planet Intro. We would have to look out for any alien spacecraft.

We were heading down into Mars' gateway taking us into the galaxy, on our way to Sparkle, the glittering planet. As we flew towards Intro, the spider planet, Savarnee and I were chatting about what we had seen.

Where had the aliens been to collect the humanoids? Had they been kidnapped or were they being bred for food like cattle? It was a strange planet, quite eerie as we passed it knowing what was going off there. It sent a shiver up our atom backs; we both felt the same as we passed. We were not sure about the use of it. We had seen no harvesting of the silk and how it could be done with the spiders being so vicious remained a mystery. They had devoured the humanoids in no time. We would not be stopping there again for a while; there was nothing waiting there but trouble. We could put that one on the back burner! Onwards and upwards – let's see what was behind those rings on Sparkle.

We were speeding along faster than ever. We wanted to discover what was hiding there and we needed to get there quickly. The faster we travelled, the more time we would have; we had never stayed out more than we dared. We did not want to overstay our welcome. We had to make sure we could return safely to Earth as we had no sustainability beyond a certain point and we were not sure where that point was. We could end up in trouble if we overstretched ourselves. We had to keep everything in perspective and not take unnecessary risks. We could not afford to make ourselves vulnerable to attack again.]

We were approaching Sparkle – Intro and Sphere were now behind us – and it was quite bright; almost blinding. As we approached Sparkle, it was like a sun in itself, casting light around the galaxy. There were strange satellites around the perimeter and they looked equipped with laser guns. They appeared like the rear lower gun turrets of a B52 Bomber from the Second World War, just orbiting the planet. But why were they there… what was their purpose? What were they guarding on the planet? Did life exist in some form? Was it the masters of the robots? Planet Sparkle was strange in its format. How deep was the space dust ring around it? Would it be an easy landing there?

There seemed to be a lot of satellites around the planet, so why were they not transmitting back to Sparkle? We could not trace any transmissions at all. We were not sure how to enter the atmosphere; it didn't seem to be like

Earth or any other of the planets. It was as if a gold, silver and platinum mesh was surrounding the planet. Was it just evolution that had created what looked like impenetrable rings? How could we access the planet's surface? We had to find a way in but something had evolved to keep aliens out of the perimeter of Sparkle. We stayed in orbit behind one of the satellites, which were 10 times larger than ours. When we rounded Sparkle, they reflected the sun in a beam of light like a welcoming beacon. They looked like they were made from a metal; possibly titanium. The sunlight seemed to be stronger than our sun and it emitted a whiter light than ours.

Was it possible that the gases were different and burned to give out more of a white light? We couldn't assess what the gases were made up of to give such a blinding light. We could only guess as it was too hot now to study, never mind going closer to it. Our mission was to discover Sparkle and its inhabitants, to see what life was living there and how advanced it would be compared to earthlings. Were we three steps ahead or five behind? We would make it our mission to find out.

We detected a spacecraft in the area. We were on red alert; we needed to make sure we had not been seen. We had to stay to the rear of the satellite. We were in a blind spot; it seemed we had learned with space and spaceships that if the satellite was equipped with cameras, they would alert spaceships to destroy us, then there would have been no hiding place. Were there spacecraft coming into the planet? Maybe there was a secret entrance through the metal dust clouds. They probably could not be penetrated by anything with an engine that needed air or gases to propel it, but maybe the technology was different here. We thought they were merely travelling to their nearest planet like Earth. We were way beyond just two planets now – we were in our new galaxy and going deeper into it.

There were three spaceships around the perimeter of Sparkle. We stayed out of sight of the spaceships; they were similar to the ones we noticed being assembled on Sphere. They seemed to be avoiding the satellites. Then, all of a sudden, we saw lasers firing at the satellites from the three spaceships; it was a full-on attack. The satellites had manoeuvred into another position to repel the attack – they spun in space, now facing the oncoming spaceships. The laser machine guns were firing bursts of beams at the spaceships, which were darting about trying to dodge the laser rays emitted from the satellites. We wondered if they were not satellites but some kind of protection system for the planet.

The spacecraft were trying to dodge the rays but it was like a game of cat and mouse. The spaceships were more on straight lines, zig-zagging, trying to outwit each other to the detriment of the other. Why would the spaceships suddenly start attacking the space defence satellites? Was this common practice? Why were they so desperate to get onto the planet to risk going against what we knew now as a defensive weapon to repel invaders?

There was obviously something there they wanted. We could see they had lasered a satellite and it was burning out in space. Suddenly, another one from an orbit below replaced the burnt-out one. The spacecraft were firing into the dust trying to make a hole to travel through into the atmosphere below. The battle was fierce; the satellites were repelling the advancing spaceships. There was space carnage everywhere. We could see a hole in the glittering dust, so we decided to go for it and hope we would be able to get out again. This was a golden opportunity to get through the defences of Sparkle.

Chapter 37

———— ◆ ————

We made a turn away from the satellite, which had detected something, possibly us, as it turned. We could see it moving towards the hole in the ring, so we darted through out of sight of the satellite. The spaceships that had attacked another area of the planet were no longer in sight as we passed through the gap in the rings. It was a large tunnel they had unknowingly blasted through the metallic rings; they had done the work for us, making a perfect hole for us to fly down. The only problem was how long it would remain open before they managed to close it. We would have to make sure that we were not going to be stranded on Sparkle and not able to leave.

We were out of transmission as we passed down through the hole so we would be in real trouble if we stayed too long. There would now be protection at the top of the hole to stop anybody else accessing the planet. It seemed they were under attack regularly to have so much security around Sparkle. We were excited as to what we would see as we entered the ozone layer. We would be able to sense what was on the surface. There was an artificial light shining through the glitter surrounding the planet. We were passing somewhere through the exosphere heading into the mesosphere and onto the stratosphere.

We had to slow our descent as we had no engines or brakes, so we could not afford to fly in too fast. We were not sure what the atmosphere was composed of –the air could be thin, making it difficult to stop as there would be no drag. We could not assume the makeup of the atmosphere would be suitable for a fast landing. We would not really know until we were in the stratosphere, then we would know how fast we would be able to descend to the planet's surface.

We were experiencing fast speeds on entry to the surface… we were not slowing down at all. It was not like the atmospheres on the other planets. It was thin air; there was no drag to slow us down, so we decided to zigzag to try and slow down. However, we were not reducing but gaining speed! We were in trouble as we were entering the stratosphere at great speed.

If we didn't slow down before the troposphere, we would be in serious trouble as we wouldn't be able to stop and would crash into the surface of the planet. Savarnee sent a distress message to base. He had no signal but hoped as it sent it would transmit to the base station.

Amanda said, "Let's try and slow this all down."

"Slow it down..." Savarnee said. "Yes, let's go back up now straight away."

Amanda said, "No, we will burn up at speed going out again."

"Not if we go up gradually. We can fly upward but at a low gradient avoiding the descent and keep it under control."

"Ok," Savarnee said, "let's do it."

Amanda took the lead and zoomed towards the mesosphere; it would be a longer way than straight down like a rocket but we had the ability to manoeuvre at will. There was no fuel so we never had to worry about running out. After all, we were atoms being fired through space; all we had to do was control speed and destination. We were way off course but we were nearly out of danger. It was a good plan by Amanda to divert and change to a horizontal ascent to eventually descend onto the planet's surface as the speed was more geared for landing.

It had been a hair-raising experience but we had got out of the situation through Amanda's quick thinking and the strategy had prevented a possible tragedy. We were on a gradual descent towards the planet's surface. We were still in dark skies and could not see the surface of the planet yet but we were close as we re-entered the stratosphere.

We encountered a flash of gold, silver and platinum rays dancing across the skies like rainbows of jewellery glittering in the skies. This was another dimension never ever seen before. We got underneath the dust and you could see turquoise lakes and rivers. As we passed over, there were trees and vegetation growing 300 feet in height. We could see the most beautiful birds flying at altitude with no signs of landing. They were so beautiful, like the rainbows had kissed their feathers with glitter. They were multi-coloured, the gold sunlight bouncing off the feathers as they flew over the trees.

What a planet this was turning out to be! We could see glittering in the lakes – there were fish, and as they swam and turned, it sent a flash of light out of the lake. As we descended further, it was grass; not green but white, and the bark on the trees was silver with titanium and gold leaves. Everything looked geared up to reflect as much light as possible. Everything about this planet was heaven and looked amazing. The colours emitted by the planet's trees, grass and lakes all complemented each other; it was an amazing place to be. We couldn't see much of life – there were some animals, gazelle and deer, but everything was glittery; the animals were multi-coloured. The sunlight Shone off their coats and it was as if someone was infatuated with glittering things.

There were multi-coloured wind clouds – we had gone through them entering the stratosphere – which seemed to join together. What was the purpose of these clouds and how could everything be living in perfect harmony? Where were the predators? Were they hiding to come out at night? The silver wind clouds were our big mystery… what was in them? They seemed so full in their shape and they were drifting over the skyline. Were they full of water ready to drop it as rain? They seemed to be an obscure shape. What were they doing travelling in the sky around the planet? We could go up through them and see what they were made up of. Gases and water vapour would be Earth's combination but these seemed to have movement of their own.

They were being propelled by some force, magnetic or other, as there was no wind on the planet. We could feel this as we roamed around the surface of the planet. There was so much we had to discover here but the issue was being able to return. With the hole mended, it might be impossible to return to the planet's surface. With all these defences in place, something here needed guarding. We would have to return later.

We talked about the spaceships attacking the glitter rings to gain entry to the atmosphere. What was it they were so desperate to find there? They obviously knew exactly what was there, and that's why they were trying to penetrate Sphere's defences. Whatever was there, they wanted it badly enough to risk spacecraft and crew who would be dying trying to penetrate the rings surrounding the planet Sparkle.

Chapter 38

W e still had to get beyond the defences ourselves to get back to Earth. We were going further now in our discovery of Unimars and its solar system. We had encountered strange worlds in dangerous situations; it was not going to be as easy as we thought. We had no defences against the satellites' ray guns; the only thing on our side was size. We were virtually invisible but that didn't mean untraceable. We had to be careful; those lasers had detected us on the way in so they could on the way out.

Given the way they destroyed the spaceships, we would not last long. One direct hit and we would be dust. We were coming out of the hole and it was heavily guarded; there was not going to be an easy way out. Amanda came up with another idea; the first one had worked so hopefully the second would. We were going to speed to the edge of the hole, but instead of shooting out, we were going to head immediately down, hugging the planet, and break out into space from an area in between the satellites. Hopefully, that way we wouldn't be detected. We had the same dilemma as the spaceships – we had to get back in to find out what was living on Sparkle. We were now on a mission to see if Amanda's strategy would work, so we zoomed out straight down. We hugged the belt of glitter staying in outer space, and soon we could see the second satellite. We had to shoot straight out now towards Sphere and past Intro back towards Mars. We couldn't get too close to the lower satellites as they would definitely see us as we were exiting.

It was busy there with laser lights all over space. There had been another attack; it had given us a way out so no one was going to see us as we sped by. It was an opportunity to get out of the outer space area into deep space. We could see the fight going off – there were at least four spaceships on fire; the hole was still there but the defence satellites had increased and the spacecraft were on a fruitless mission. They were not going to penetrate Sparkle's defence systems.

Amanda said, "No wonder they're having to make so many spaceships. It makes you wonder what other planets they are attacking. Is it just a case of making the galaxy theirs?" Why would they try to get to somewhere that was impregnable? It was not happening and the spacecraft were burning up and making it a potential junkyard, although they always came down burning up in the atmosphere.

We had passed space junk on our journey and had to avoid it. There were so many lasers lighting space up giving us light to navigate by and we could see Sphere in the distance. It was still light; there was no dark space here as the bright sun lit space completely. There was nowhere to hide until we got beyond Sphere. We tried a zigzag approach as the war was continuing and there would be spaceships moving in to take part in the invasion of Sparkle. We actually wanted to help defend Sparkle from being invaded. We had seen the spaceship factories on Sphere and the speed at which they assembled them was frightening. In open space, they would probably be able to detect us. We could not take risks; we would have to fly lower than the planet to ensure safe passage home.

We could see more spaceships leaving Sphere on their way to Sparkle. There would be no peace today for the planet's defences on Sparkle. They would be tested to the maximum where the spaceships were attacking, trying to put as many holes as possible in the atmosphere of Sparkle until they had a clear passage through to the ground. Maybe we could give the co-ordinates to base and they could try and laser the spaceships but would we be bringing the war to us on Earth, alerting the attacking forces to our presence and our planet itself? They seemed to be able to defend the planet and replace the defences, but where would it all end? Possibly only when the invading forces had taken it over.

We were rounding Mars; not long back to base. We had communication with base and said all was well and we would discuss our discoveries when we got back. We did not want any aliens picking up our transmissions. As small as we were, it was a sure bet they could trace the signal; they appeared to be relentless in their attack. It could only be detrimental to Earth to have contact with an invading force. They were never going to give up the battle for Sparkle, and we were not in any position to help them.

We had no idea what, besides the animals and birds, were living there. Were there any humanoids, or something that would appear to be alien in its form? We did not think that the planets could sustain human life as we know it.

We were now coming through Earth's atmosphere and would soon be back at base. It had been a good flight and we had encountered many things on this mission. It was exciting but only due to the danger we might be in from Earth's perspective. We were pioneers in space and relentless in our pursuit of the discovery of new worlds.

We had arrived at base with no sign of trouble entering the atmosphere. We were down and getting ready to go home. Tomorrow, we had to all work on the laser weapon as we could not afford to keep going on missions without backup. It was nearly ready to be fired into space on our next mission, its final testing before making it permanently active. It would only be able to do short distances – possibly to the planets in our galaxy and our new discovery, Unimars.

We were all geared up and tooled up to finish off the laser weapon. There was some work to do on the distance to make sure it was deadly accurate as it would have to be able to ensure it would hit only the target set and not veer off and hit one of our own team.

"We will possibly have to inform the US military we have the weapon and need to use it," Amanda said.

The team all said, "No, we can deal with this ourselves."

Amanda said, "We will all be in trouble."

Adam said, "We are already up to our necks in trouble! We need to do this on our own and keep the secret we have already. We can't afford for the authorities to find out. How can we possibly explain our actions here?"

We needed to finish off the laser as our missions were getting more dangerous every trip. We needed to know why the people in the spaceships needed to invade Sparkle, what were they after and why it was guarded so fiercely. It could only be that they wanted the minerals the planet had, but what minerals would it have there? Unlike Sphere and Intro, there appeared to be no population, so where did the humanoids come from to feed the spiders, and were they also food for other planets in the galaxy?

We were all guessing but we were sure we would find all the answers soon. Adam and Anthony would be the team now going, while Blaise, Amanda and Savarnee would be here to test the weapon. Blaise wanted to go on the mission, however, we said we needed his knowledge to be able to set the computer on the laser ensuring it would be deadly accurate So that we knew we could destroy any alien forces that came near Earth. If they did, it would need to work beyond Mars to ensure distance between us and invading aliens, providing the laser would track its target; we would have to put it to the test. There would be nobody on a mission to an alien planet today; it was just to Mars to see the results of our work on the weapon.

Once we had it working, there would be no alien invasion of Earth. We had to pick out some co-ordinates on Mars and try to hit the spot. Adam and Anthony would have to travel to Mars and mark the targets for the laser to fire at. It would have to be so accurate if we were going to one day be able to use it as a weapon against the invaders of Sparkle.

We would be on an early start in the laboratory in the morning. The team said the laser was ready so all we had to do was turn in a short trip to Mars and, if successful, we could move on knowing we had a weapon to defend us.

Chapter 39

———◆———

Morning came fast and we were on our way. Anthony and Adam would be close to the co-ordinates selected by Blaise and they would be looking to see if the laser hit the target area the team had set. Adam had taken the lead, with Anthony coming up behind him. Adam thought they would be less conspicuous that way. There were going to be bright lights from the laser as it would fire in bursts rather than a straight-line continuous beam; it would be too far to expect that. We were going to have to be able to bend the beam so it would round Mars into the gateway to the galaxy Unimars.

It was frustrating that we couldn't have the technology and the materials to build spaceships like the aliens on Sphere. We would need their spiders' webs for the heat-shields and need to know how they powered their space-ships, but for now, this was the only way to travel. We were learning more every day about the planets here; there seemed to be no lack of space or overpopulation. We were ready and at a place near to where the laser target was. We

231

had three sites to hit, however, we were not sure how far away we would have to be to be out of danger. We could be the target if the laser bent or went off course. We would be burnt to a crisp! We had to make sure we were close enough to see the target without *becoming* the target.

We were in position and sent a message to the team. As we finished the conversation, we could see the burst of laser shots coming towards Mars. They were so bright they must have seen them leaving from Earth's spy stations. The Hubble was always disabled during take-off and landing; they must have had 24-hour maintenance people there as we turned it off every mission. The laser was forming a line as it was being fired, the bursts catching up with each other. They were heading for Mars and looked on target. As they hit Mars, all we saw was a bright light and fire. It was the best firework display we had seen; the surface of Mars being lifted into space by the laser.

The planet area was on fire from the laser; it had melted the rock and dust that lay on the planet. It was accurate to the millimetre. No spaceship would have been able to absorb an impact so severe; it was more deadly than a nuclear bomb. It had even sent a mushroom-shaped cloud into space.

"I don't think it would be wise to test it again," Adam said.

"Hey, man," Anthony blurted out, "bloody good show though."

Adam contacted base and told them about the debris but it was a direct hit.

Amanda said, "Well, let's do one more hit in the same spot. We can do a reset on the laser computer so it's firing a new target but at the same area. It might not do so much damage to Mars causing less debris."

"Ok," Adam said. "Let's do it."

We remained in the same position as Amanda fired.

"Wow, here it comes!" Anthony said.

Adam replied, "The laser hit the rock that hard with such force it seems to be melting the rock and leaving a large hole."

We could have driven a truck through after the laser had finished. It was still red-hot; we could see the molten rock dripping into the large hole.

The power must have been immense. Whatever Blaise and Anthony had done, it was so accurate and powerful that it would be our safety net against any aggression against us.

We would just need to make sure Blaise could program the laser to bend around Mars like an arc down the gateway into Unimars and hit the target we had selected the co-ordinates for. It would be a ticket to going further into the galaxy. At least we had some defence as long as we were in an area where we could contact base. Something was better than nothing. We were just pioneers, not an invading force as we had no weapon we could carry. But we had a clear run into Sparkle. We were hopefully going to find some alien life there and find out what the planet was defending.

On tomorrow's mission, we were going to visit Sparkle, so we needed to gain access before the hole was repaired. They had not recognised us so we were fairly safe to go. We did not want to hurt them in any way, just to make friends with an alien nation and teach or learn from them.

Amanda and Savarnee would be on the mission. It was a good combination as Amanda would keep Savarnee close to her as he was a bit reckless in his pursuit of space. Everything had to happen in its own time; no room in space for a reckless person who could endanger the team, but he was good at what he did. I felt safe to have him around. He was fast in his reactions and always alert, so a good member of the team to have with me on today's mission.

We were having to go to Sparkle now as there would be a chance to get in before they closed up the hole in the glitter rings surrounding the planet. We had to get onto the surface and look around. We would have time to explore the strange clouds we had been told about. We were on our way. Savarnee said he was excited to be coming on this mission of discovery. We had rounded Mars, speeding down the gateway and towards Unimars. We could see Intro in front of us; all seemed calm – no alien spaceships anywhere to be seen. We passed Sphere and all seemed quiet; it didn't look like there were any missions from them today.

They were waging war on Sparkle but the planet had really good defensive capabilities. They had done well with the satellites patrolling the orbit around the planet; it seemed they had definitely got an impregnable outer layer. We just had to be the ones to get through it. We could see the hole was nearly stitched back together and was looking impregnable again. We would only have a short time; we would have to be in and out as fast as possible. We were close to the outer rings, now heading towards the hole. We had followed the lead of Adam and Anthony and crawled up underneath. We were small enough to hide in between the layers of the glitter rings and make our way up towards the hole. We were inside the first layer of glitter; it was like going through a tunnel made of gold mesh.

It was blinding to travel through it. Although could see, we could also feel the brightness as we travelled towards the hole. We would have to make sure we were not detected. We were nearing the hole, yet, as we got there, we could see robots stitching it back together. They had four arms that were symmetrical down the front of the body; different hands for different jobs. We stopped just in sight of them, but they seemed to be programmed to work without intervention from any overseers.

It seemed the planets in Unimars all employed robotic skills and they seemed to be put to work on all tasks. It was amazing watching the way they stitched it back together. It was not gold braid; it was somewhere between that and a cloud – virtually invisible. They were tying the two together to form a mesh, and it was the gases that made it glitter. We could not make out the makeup of the finished mesh cloud but it was effective at keeping out any uninvited guests. We were brushing up against it; the cloud was soft but it had substance. We couldn't define it yet but there must have been ways for access in both directions.

Chapter 40

———◆———

We managed to get beyond the edge into the hole and speed down to the surface unnoticed. There seemed to be no defences on the planet itself… it was such a beautiful place. There were white swan-like birds on the turquoise lakes; the grass was white, but everything was colourful. The bark on the trees was in shades of blue; the foliage on them was fur-like, in lighter blues and white floss. The birds flying overhead had four wings and a fanned tail as they flew from tree to tree. We could see silver fish as large as dolphins swimming in the water, the light glistening off them as they turned to play.

This had all been set out like a paradise planet. Everything was put there to raise your expectations on what paradise would be like. There seemed to be everything here you would expect to see in heaven. We thought we would stay and discover more and hoped we could get back out through the hole later. We observed a landing craft, silent in its approach, come down to the lake and two aliens exited the door. They were walking; their feet appeared to be twice as large as a human, their hands were more like claws on a crab and their torsos were shell-like with crustaceans on them as if they lived in the ocean.

Maybe they could have come from the sea. The heads were scaly and the mouth was puckered up like a fish. Their eyes were as black as coal with a sharp silver horizontal insert and they walked with bent legs looking like they were ready to jump somewhere. They were fairly scary with their layered scales building up a large head three times the size of a human.

They seemed to have laser guns in a silver steel belt across the chest at the front. As we waited, they stopped and made a screeching noise and the back of the shell opened up and two wings came out. They flapped at hummingbird speed and the aliens took off above the trees towards the silver clouds. We wondered where they were going and why they had evolved the way they had. We could see them inspecting the clouds as they flew around them. What interest did the clouds hold for them? Could we mimic these creatures and fool them into thinking we were all one?

There would have to be more so we could mingle amongst them and find out what they were doing here. Had they evolved or were they sent here to work on the planet's vegetation and maintain what was hiding in the silver clouds above? If we could find more of these aliens, we could mimic them and try to find out what this planet Sparkle was all about. It seemed like paradise; everything was perfect here, but why were the spaceships trying to break down the defences of the glitter rings?

Savarnee said, "Let's move on a bit around the planet and see if it's more populated somewhere else."

So, we moved on. We could see lights in the distance a long way off but were able to get there. We could see the clouds as we passed looking so full; whatever was in them was a mystery to us. We just wanted to know why they looked so full as they streamed around the atmosphere. We would have to wait to see.

Savarnee said, "Can we not fly into them to see what's in there?"

"No," Amanda said. "It's not really our business. Let's see if we can find out another way. If we can infiltrate a crowd, we may be able to imitate two of them and get to know all about what they are doing here and they might tell us what is in the clouds above."

Savarnee said, "You have your wish!"

We flew towards the lights and saw there were hundreds of aliens all lying flat down on the white grass with their legs and arms spread out, touching each other, connecting all their parts in a star-like pattern. There were five connected to make the star. They were symmetrical in their positioning and covered a large area of land. They seemed to be submissive to a superior force, probably forcing them to worship them in this way.

It would be a good opportunity to infiltrate them after their worship. Were they that much different to us, even though they were hundreds of millions of miles away? We could see the star-like linkages that had formed were breaking up as a high-pitched siren came on; it must have meant the prayers were finished. They seemed subservient but they gave an idea they were a gentle race of aliens. They had been put there for a purpose; they did not seem as if they were native to the planet. Sparkle seemed more adapted to angels sitting around in circles playing their harps. The place was amazing.

Amanda said, "This is where I want to be one day when it's my turn to go to heaven."

Savarnee said, "Me too. It's so tranquil, I could stay here forever. It's not busy and overcrowded like Earth. We can move and breathe here. It's paradise like no other place. Let's try and mimic and fit in around them and see what we can learn."

We transformed ourselves. Savarnee looked at Amanda and laughed; she looked so different but a perfect match. We would have to stay together or we would lose each other; it seemed it was easy to move between them. Nobody seemed to have a specific job to do, just to be there. If they were needed, they were all carers and care-takers doing a job keeping the planet immaculate in its conception. We were curious as to what was above us in the clouds. We really had prioritised our need to know. We were out to get as much information as we could and we would have to obtain it from the workers. We managed to pick up some of the language and we could see by their actions and passing signs onto others that we could find out what could be up there by pointing or other signs.

Savarnee said he had a good idea how to communicate with them. His father was deaf and he had learned sign language so was good at displaying signs with his hands and moving his mouth, pronouncing the words without knowing how they sounded to a person that had good hearing. It seemed these beings were not able to communicate with sound so Savarnee said he could understand some of the signs and noises they made. This was beyond me so I thought I would leave it to Savarnee to try communicating with them. He was really good and they were trying to chat back. He was trying to make out that he was shortsighted and could not always decipher the messages they were trying to get across. This was giving him time to absorb the language they were speaking. Pointing up to the clouds, he said a word I didn't understand but they did point up to the clouds as well.

Savarnee was making all the right sounds but we were running out of time. We needed to get back before we were locked in. If the robots finished fast, we would not be going out again and we could not be away from our bodies or we would be in trouble. So, no matter how important it seemed to know about what was happening here, we could not stay longer than our remit. We would have to make tracks to get out on time and get back.

Savarnee said, "In the last conversation, they were holding their heads and pointing to the other side of their heads. I was not sure what they were talking about; it seemed like it was something inside their head they wanted to tell me."

Chapter 41

———— ♦ ————

Were they thinking about the clouds or was it in their head? We had to go; we could pick up again on Savarnee's next visit.

We just managed to get through the hole into outer space. They had filled it quickly; the only way we could possibly get in again would be behind the cover of another attack by the spaceships. We could probably get in the hole that had been made by their lasers; probably too small for them to get in but definitely the right size for us. For now, we would report back to base and see what they all made of what we had discovered.   Savarnee would be the key to opening up what was being carried so preciously in the silver clouds. We could only return with Savarnee as his sign language had opened doors that we couldn't have opened but it was something to do with the aliens' heads. Was it possibly head trauma? Were there some problems with aliens here? Savarnee was struggling to find out what was there. We would have to wait until we could get in, but next time, it would be trial and error to be able to get through the defence system into Sparkle again.

We were on our way back to Earth; it had been an eye-opener; especially meeting the aliens and being able to mimic them. They seemed quiet, subdued and were totally focused on the work they carried out. It had given Savarnee an advantage of a regular place at Sparkle as he was the only one of us who knew sign language fluently.

Amanda said to him, "You have an unfair advantage on us all."

Laughing, Savarnee replied, "Yeah, you could be right!"

We could see Earth as we rounded Mars. What news we had for the team! We would be having a meeting the next morning for a brief on what would be the next move on Sparkle. We would be chatting in the morning; the rest of the team had been tweaking the laser weapon and we would be testing its ability to track a target, even to negotiate around other sides of planets and into other galaxies like Unimars. We had to be able to use it for defence whilst we were discovering Unimars. It was a large galaxy and protection would be paramount on our discovery missions.

Blaise said, "It is ready to try."

He had re-chipped it to recognise the tracker chip and, providing the co-ordinates were correct, it would hit the target fully tracked. We would look at a strike on the other side of Mars on our next trip. We would all be waiting to see the results of the test as we needed to work to ensure all our teams' safety. We were all feeling more confident now we had the laser weapon.

Blaise had done well adapting it all to work as a weapon. The weekend was here so Monday would be the next day to explore Sparkle if we could find a way in through the glitter rings. Savarnee was aware of where the last entry and exit had been, so at least it wouldn't be a wasted mission if we couldn't infiltrate Sparkle's defence. We had to give co-ordinates for the laser test on the rear of Mars. We would also have to wait to ensure the target had been hit and that it was accurate.

Monday was here so fast and we were off and nearing Mars. All seemed to be ok; no problems. We were communicating back to base. All was ready with the laser. We would just have to position ourselves in the right place at the right distance away where we could still see the target area without becoming the target. We would have to be vigilant because, when that ray came in bursts, we did not want to be near it. As it came around Mars, we had to trust Blaise had got it right and it wouldn't be seeking any other target, mainly us.

Blaise transmitted, "We're ready to fire the weapon. Can you give the exact co-ordinates?"

Savarnee sent a message.

Blaise replied, "Ok, got them. Watch out – I'm sending the laser."

We were clear of Mars, looking in from outer space, so we could see the beam from Earth leaving the bursts of light at lightning speed coming towards us.

They had reached us in a split second. They were aimed at Mars, coming towards us… Was it going to turn or was it like a torpedo looking for a target? It was too late; it was too fast to see but the light trail showed it had rounded the back of Mars and we could see burning on the surface. It had worked; it hit the target! The laser had made a hole in Mars. It was so powerful it was unbelievable how deep the hole was. It was a formidable weapon. It would probably not be so accurate at longer distances but it was incredible as a weapon to remove any invading force.

It would incinerate them from millions of miles away. I don't think they would come again; Earth is a safer place today than it was yesterday. We had the capability of defending ourselves, so now we would be a formidable enemy against some alien attack.

We were on our way to Sparkle; we had made good time and, hopefully, we would be able to access Sparkle through the glitter rings around it. We would have to be careful of the satellite defences which were going 24 hours a day. There was no time off for them; they had to be on guard indefinitely. We would have to do what Amanda said and go underneath them and hug Sparkle's glitter rings until we could find a hole to access the surface through the atmosphere.

It would now be a task to find a way into the outer layer and to the surface of Sparkle. We needed to be able to find out what was in the silver clouds. We had taken inquisitive to a new level. We had to gain access to what seemed to be the secret of Sparkle; second-best information would not be acceptable. Savarnee was making headway but we were all looking for answers. The team were all excited about what we would find. We were hugging the glitter rings looking for a way in – there had to be one or how would anybody be able to travel in and out of Sparkle?

We were looking for some secret door into the atmosphere of Sparkle. We flew around the planet avoiding the satellite detectors. We were just specks, although they turned a few times and made us sweat – well, after a fashion. We would have trouble sweating as we were just atoms but still vulnerable to attack as they would not be sure of our intentions. We could be scouts for a larger attack force. If they only knew our capabilities, they would welcome us with open arms. We were for the defence of

Sparkle against the spaceship attacks. We were looking for a way in underneath the planet when we saw a small craft exit the planet; the area it came out of closed up as it left.

"Did you see that?" Savarnee messaged Adam.

"Yeah, I have the co-ordinates. Let's put them in and see if we can get in where they came out. They must have a detection system to see if it's clear of spaceships before they exit or enter Sparkle."

"Let's go for it," Savarnee messaged.

"Yeah," Adam said, "let's go."

We sped up to the area. We could see no opening but knew there was something in the glitter rings that was just a shade off-colour. We would go for it and see if it was our way into Sparkle. We could access the impossible so we were going for it.

"Sparkle, here we come!" Adam said.

It was a bit scary going in through the glitter rings. We did not know what we would meet as we went in… would it be closely guarded? We were not sure if two small atoms going in would cause a fuss –hopefully, we were virtually invisible anyway as we flew into the glitter rings.

They opened slightly like a curtain to let us through! It was strange – we never expected the glitter ring to open its defences so easily. It was as if they were expecting us to come in and the door was wide open for us. We were going to have to proceed with caution as we did not know what to expect. We left the outer space and were making our way through a large tunnel towards the planet's surface. We could see the surface in front of us… but something was different. It was a mirror image of the surface. We were not going to be able to go straight down – we were being diverted into a large holding chamber.

What had we come into? It seemed the hole was closing up behind us and we were being guided into a vast chamber, big enough for a spaceship. Was this a trap? There was no way out and we could only go forward. Had we been discovered infiltrating their planet? What was the likely outcome going to be? We were in trouble but how much would soon be determined. We had come so far and learned very little about space and its frontiers, where to go and where not to. We probably had been running before we could walk. As we looked around, we could sense danger as there were lasers everywhere.

This whole area was automated, there was nobody in sight, so although we had stumbled into a dangerous area, how dangerous could it be? We were not sure about our next five minutes never mind our future. If we died, we would not have a future; possibly our brains would die with us. We had to find a way out of this chamber we were in, but it was totally self-contained. There was no security, no automatic communications; it was just a holding chamber fully secured. Our only problem was that coming through the glitter ring activated the closure behind us, so we were going to have trouble getting out.

Chapter 42

————— ♦ —————

We would have to keep a low profile whilst we scouted about looking for an exit or a way onto the planet's surface so we could possibly find a way out from there. We had stumbled into a dark place with very little chance of getting out. We would probably die here if we couldn't find a way through the tunnel to outer space. We were really concerned we had no signal back to base; we were on our own. No back-up; no nothing. Nobody even knew we had found a way in through the glitter rings. We were well and truly in a mess; we would have to wait it out. We had just about given up hope of getting out when a door, which had been totally invisible, opened from the front of the chamber and out came the space shuttle.

"That's the one on the planet!" Savarnee said. "Let's hope it's leaving – we can tag along behind it."

Adam said, "Yes, let's follow it out. We can wait until it passes and get up right behind it. I just hope there are no sensors on it to be able to know we are behind it."

The craft got to the tunnel and it opened.

Adam said, "Come on. So far, so good."

On its approach, the spaceship increased speed to exit the tunnel. We had to keep up as we couldn't afford the tunnel entrance to close before we were through it. We had plenty of power but we had been caught napping, and effectively, we were getting left behind. We had to move fast to catch up. As the shuttle was exiting through the outer hole, we were right up there behind them.

Adam said to Savarnee, "Make sure you head straight down and hug the glitter ring until the space shuttle has disappeared."

The hole to outer space shut so fast as we came out, that if we hadn't been right up their rear, we would have crashed into the glitter door as it closed and possibly terminated ourselves as atoms.

We would have to tell the team about this; they would have to know everything we had encountered today. It was definitely an experience; we were so glad to be on the way back.

As we came up to our level for travel back to Earth, we set a course for Sphere. We were cruising all the way back; we had been in a bad place in the chamber and we were breathing a sigh of relief. We had to make sure there would be a way out, so it would be good if we could time it to coincide with the movements of the space shuttle. It seemed that a maintenance vehicle also paid daily visits to Sparkle. We could hide underneath and wait for it to arrive and come up fast to follow it in.

Once we were in, we could let the shuttlecraft go ahead and follow it discreetly into the chamber and then onto the planet's surface. We would have to ensure we followed the craft back out through the chamber and back to outer space. There could be no lock-ins for us – we had never been away long enough to test how the brains would cope with the added time zones, and the energy source emitted could be diminished and we would just be space dust floating around the galaxy. We were passing Sphere and we counted seven spaceships leaving the planet. We slowed as they passed above us. Were they heading for Sparkle? They had turned on a trajectory for Sparkle, so it looked like it was going to be an attack force against Sparkle's defence.

Savarnee said, "Let's follow them and see what's happening."

Adam said, "No, we have to get back; we're out of time already. We need to make tracks back to Earth."

We wondered if Sparkle's defences would hold out in a full-on attack. Why would they keep on attacking? What were the invading force after on Sparkle? It seemed a strange place of beauty. Were they invading for resources the planet may hold, like gold or platinum or other raw materials? They probably needed the raw materials to make compounds to build the spaceships.

We wanted to help Sparkle defend against the aggressors from Sphere but it was not our war to fight, and what right would we have to take sides? How did we know what was happening? It could be Sphere that was defending itself against Sparkle. We had not been around the other side of Sparkle so we had no idea – there could be a military base around there attacking Sphere. We needed more information. Why was Sparkle so heavily guarded by the robotic satellites? Why so many of them? The planet was heavenly; why would anybody attack it?

We had to know more; we couldn't move on until we had discovered why it was being targeted by Sphere spaceships. We were going to have to discuss if we dared help out Sparkle against the attacking forces; after all, we had the tracker laser. We would be able to eliminate any invading force on Sparkle as well as Earth. our thoughts were that it would end in a galaxy war where planets would be at risk. We would be ok in our galaxy, but it seemed most of the planets had no way of sustaining life.

We were back at base and back in the laboratory. The subject now was Sparkle and protecting the planet against attack from the spaceships from Sphere. Were they just warring neighbours? Had they fallen out about something? All manner of thoughts were going through our heads as to why they were being attacked by the spaceships.

They seemed relentless in their pursuit of Sparkle. We had to help Sparkle out; it was unfair that they should suffer persistent attacks. We could not be party to it. We all agreed there was a possibility they could attack us next for interfering with their business.

Amanda questioned what right we could have to kill people from another world because they were attacking a neighbouring planet. Was that an act of war or just the norm to war with your neighbours? Sparkle looked like it could look after itself, so there would be no need for help. We needed to find out why a planet of people would go to war. What could be so bad that it had come to this? We were going to have a full investigation into what was happening on Sparkle but we would have to be able to access our defence system in place if we needed to defend ourselves.

We had decided not to use the laser for anything without the permission of the government and world leaders. We were at risk but we had gone into their domain. Three months ago, nobody would have known anything about Unimars and the planets within the galaxy.

It would be Anthony going with Savarnee tomorrow; they knew the risks which were getting more intense every day. We were trying to get around their security systems and that would never be a good option as they were heavily defended. The guys knew the risks and they were ready for whatever was coming. They would have to take on Sphere as well as Sparkle because they were invaders in space and had no right to anything.

We had to try and follow the shuttle in and out and could not afford the chance of being seen. We would have to be so obscure that nobody would know we had been. We were ready to visit Unimars, see what the galaxy held out for us, and find out why the galaxy was so bright with its sun and two moons. Why did it have more than our galaxy? Perhaps the Milky Way wasn't bright enough and that was why we were the only life force visible.

Chapter 43

———————◆———————

Ours seemed to be a barren galaxy – either it was dead or not fully evolved enough to sustain life, with our planet still young in its form and still cooling down from the Big Bang that scientists say happened. So, were we all still evolving instead of being a dead galaxy? We would be the ones to find out. Meanwhile, Unimars seemed alive and this was taking our attention away from our own galaxy. Nothing seemed to be interesting enough for us to visit other planets in our own galaxy. We were out to conquer planets, and eventually, our goal would be to discover new species on new planets in new galaxies.

We had the best team ever; we could invent and produce virtually anything we needed. We were a mix of different professions but everything worked perfectly together. What we didn't know we could research and put together. We were the best in our fields of work.

Anthony and Savarnee were going out today. The idea was that they would wait and follow the shuttlecraft in and then out later and that would give Savarnee enough time to communicate with the aliens of Sparkle to find out what was so important to the spaceships of Sphere that they would risk so much against the defences of Sparkle – hopefully we would know soon. We had to infiltrate with the aliens to try and extract some information.

The cloning worked really well. No one was suspicious of us. They probably thought we were not able to speak and would do their best to understand us, thinking we were one of the same. We just needed to get in through Sparkle's defences without us being the target. We would do the same as before. Savarnee was an old hand in all this now; it was his third time. They had to make it work since there was still too much to see. We could not spend too much time on Sparkle as we still had so many planets in this galaxy to see and discover.

As we came towards the planet, there were bright lights in the dark of space. There was another attack happening, and, as we rounded Sphere, we could see it all going off. There was a large spaceship defending the position; the spaceships from Sphere were attacking to their detriment. The large ship had armaments all over it, machine-gun-type lasers firing explosive beams out of it, taking out the spaceships like they were made of wood. No space-ship could outrun or out-gun this attack spaceship; it was something from another world completely. Savarnee called it the Doomsday Machine; it was awesome. The fire power was unbelievable.

It was definitely the widow-maker. All those people on the spaceships were being obliterated by this weapon. You could not call it a spaceship… more the terminator of the galaxy. This had been sent in to destroy every spaceship that threatened. Death had come to space in this awesome master of the cosmos. This was definitely the pinnacle of spaceships, terrifying to even look at. This was a real battleship, armour-plated with panels of steel-type material covering its exterior. Sphere was never going to out-gun it; Sparkle had called in the reserves and the spaceships from Sphere were effectively running for the hills as we would say.

Anything in front of this monster, perfectly described, would be instantly incinerated by the armoured lasers; just one hit… that was all it needed. We saw one spaceship trying to get away and it was reduced to space dust in less than a split second. Not only was this a deadly monster, it was also extremely accurate.

All the spaceships were trying to exit Sparkle's outer space. There weren't many going back to Sphere, and those that made it out were all limping back; they had met more than their match. We saw the back of the battleship open and it started sucking all the damaged spaceships into the rear hold. We could see sparks coming out the back – it seemed they were being chewed up and deposited into some kind of recycling bin for spaceships.

We thought about the people who would be still alive in the destroyed spaceships being mangled up in the recycle bin at the rear of the war machine. There was going to be no mercy for any invaders. These were part of a space clean now they had met the Doomsday Machine. It was not a good outcome for them; there was a lot of carnage so it must have been a full-on attack on Sparkle. That war machine was quickly cleaning up the bodies and souls of the aliens that had died in the battle. It didn't make any sense to keep on attacking Sparkle, whatever it was they were desperate to obtain.

They were relentless in their attacks on Sparkle, however, they were not expecting the doomsday spaceship to be there and defend Sparkle so efficiently.

"What will our fate be?" we thought.

Savarnee said, "If we are caught, will they see us as an enemy and deal with us?"

Anthony said, "Hey, man, no mercy for us; just a trip into the recycle bin." Anthony laughed.

Savarnee said, "Well, I'm not ready for the recycling bin."

Anthony said, "Hey, man, live with it."

"Live with it…" Savarnee replied. "I'm not ready for that bin yet!"

Anthony said, "Hey, man, you will be off for a ride in the bin."

Savarnee said, "Let's forget it and move on. Let's wait for the shuttle and go in and mingle with the locals and see if we can find out what's in those clouds."

"Hey, man," Anthony replied, "let's go."

It was just a short time before the shuttle arrived. It appeared to slow down to look at what was happening in outer space. It could see the Doomsday Machine was still doing its cleaning; it was moving around the planet out of sight.

The coast was clear for us to enter Sparkle, so we made our way down to the door under the planet.

"Stay close, Anthony," Savarnee transmitted. "We are good to go."

"Yeah, man," Anthony replied.

We came down the tunnel towards the chamber; it was really dark but we could find our way through a muddy pond in the black of night. We were sensing our way through. We had no eyes; just an amazing sensory ability that the brains were projecting. We could sense the shuttle moving out of the chamber. The other door had opened and we were travelling in behind the shuttle. We would be able to stay right behind it so we could not be seen or sensed. Suddenly, we darted out from behind the space shuttle – we had seen what appeared to be a small city.

Chapter 44

———◆———

All white in colour, it seemed everything here was made to look so tranquil; it was paradise. There was nothing there to cause anybody any harm. We had the ability to transform into an image that could fool them into believing we were one of the same. We could see the alien species walking around so we transformed ourselves to their image, mingling in as we mixed with them. They were sitting in the park areas; it seemed to be so relaxed and nothing seemed hurried.

It was 25 degrees and there were only silver clouds; there were no dark ones or clear blue skies. Everything here was white – the sky, the buildings, the grass… The trees looked wonderful, with their colours all pastel. This place was like nowhere else but the beings were a wonderful species. They talked and walked together; lots were holding hands. They were so gentle and had no clue what was happening up there in outer space and the carnage that was being collected by the war machine. They were protected from all of that, but what force was in place to protect these beings and where was it coming from?

Was it based on the planet somewhere, or was the Doomsday Machine brought in from somewhere to protect Sparkle when the satellites were being out-gunned? We had to find out the information we had come for – the secret to what they were hiding inside the clouds floating around in the sky. It was our mission to find out from the local aliens what was in the clouds. Savarnee was on it; he was already in the crowd using sign language. He looked like he was making headway as they were looking up to the clouds and they were pointing things out.

We had to keep a certain distance as we were not matter but just a projection of light and colour, however, we could communicate and that was what we needed to be able to do more than anything else. Savarnee was getting so good with the communication that they were giving away a lot of information about the planet and its residents. They were just adults; no children here. I wanted to know what Savarnee had found out – they were pointing to their heads like there was something wrong with their ears. Savarnee was pointing up and trying to get them to tell him what was in the clouds floating around the sky. I could see Savarnee kept pointing to his own head and twirling his fingers around in a circular motion. It was a sign that they had problems carrying out tasks and were unable to communicate properly.

He was starting to get some response and they were pointing to different parts of his head; he was tapping on the front of his head as they spoke about the spaceships coming down onto the base of the planet. They must have had some near misses. Possibly the spaceships from Sphere had got down to the ground of Sparkle. They must have known what was going off. They were moving their arms around – it was difficult to understand when they could move all four arms at once, so coordinating was natural to them but an absolute nightmare to him.

I mimicked with one of our arms raising an arm up, telling him it was time to leave. Savarnee got the message. I could see him waving his arms about and virtually touching the aliens in a farewell gesture. We both turned the corner and we had dissolved into atoms again; we were ready to go. We had to follow the shuttlecraft out or we would be trapped here; we had no clue what triggered the doors leading to the chamber. We had no idea when it would be leaving, but it would probably leave at the same time as yesterday. We were late and we would have to make time up if we were going out with the shuttle. We could see the aliens making their way to it, so we speeded up and came in behind them.

We were on our way back – just a trip to the chamber and then up the tunnel out of the atmosphere into outer space. We travelled up to the chamber only to find another space shuttle parked up, suspended, waiting for work to be done. There were robots working on it, much like the robots on Sphere. We could not afford to be seen and there was nowhere to hide; we would be visible to the robots working on the spaceship.

They seemed to be able to repair the space shuttle with no programming. They appeared to be replacing parts only, not repairing them, and they seemed to clip on and off. All the wearable items must have been on the outsides of the shuttle. For some reason, we were docking at the side of them. Nothing was visible but the robots were already working on the shuttle.

Anthony said, "Let's get over the top of the shuttle."

As we came over the top, luckily for us the space shuttle stopped and hovered above the shuttle being mended. We could see them but they could not see us. We would need to ensure, when the space shuttle moved, that we were not blown off into the view of the windows in the other craft, otherwise, we could be spotted.

As we were talking, some sirens came on and the shuttle started to move, but not forward. It was moving up and we were right on top for everybody to see. We either had to wait there and hope we were not seen, or try and get off the top to the back.

Anthony said, "Let's stay – if they see us, we can just outrun them."

Savarnee said, "How's that then? How the hell are we going to get out of here without the shuttle opening the curtain door of Sparkle's rings?"

"Yeah, man," Anthony said "Never thought about that; let's go behind but stay more in the middle of the shuttlec- raft – it will make more sense. We can move up or down as we are passing the other one. The last thing we need is to be caught here."

We would not be able to explain our reasons for being there and that would be difficult. We would be caught in a net and then taken into a laboratory for examination. They would never believe who we were and where we came from – being captured had always been our fear. We would be seen as an experiment rather than prisoners; we were nothing but an atom out of our brains. We had evolved that way; that our brains were superior to other aliens, although not capable of travelling with matter.

It would be a long time before we had the technology of the spaceships of Sphere. The robots were doing a fast build of them and they were effective, but no match for the war machine. The doomsday spacecraft, the widow-maker we had named it, had earned its name; it had totally annihilated the whole fleet of spaceships from Sphere. The technology on the war machine must have been mind-blowing.

Chapter 45

———— ◆ ————

W e had started up the gateway. We had maintained silence with base as we could be giving away our positions if they could triangulate the signal and they would be able to pinpoint our position and capture or destroy us so it was imperative not to use communications whilst in Unimars. Once we were rounding Mars, we could call base as it was a straight road back to Earth.

We were well on our way and we told the team what had happened. Savarnee just wanted to get back and gather all the information they had told him and try and put it together. All the hand signals and pointing – it had to mean something, They were not exiled for nothing. There was more here than we could imagine; the defences were too much to have nothing.

Savarnee was thinking and putting everything together on the way back to Earth. We were all having a meeting with the bosses in the morning as we could not give away our missions. We had all voted to keep it secret and we did not want anybody bailing out. there was little chance of that as we wanted to be pioneers of space and nothing was going to change that. It was all exciting, every day, especially now there was always something going off. We would let Savarnee think about all that he had learned from his conversation so we parted until the morning.

We arrived two hours earlier so we could find out what Savarnee had managed to extract from the local aliens. We sat down around the table; it was a reality board meeting and we needed a full explanation from Savarnee on this cloud subject. When Savarnee started to talk, the team were all ears.

"Well, what I've found out is nothing." The team looked up.

"Nothing?" Adam shouted over.

Savarnee just held onto his composure.

"Nothing," he said.

"That's ridiculous," Amanda said. "Hey, man," Anthony said, "no way."

Blaise muttered.

Savarnee said, "Well, ok, I found out loads."

The team all jeered him calling him a fake.

Savarnee said, "Ok then, but I was the only one that could have got the information. I've had a bit of pressure to produce the findings; I've been up all night trying to put it together. I think I've got it... unless I'm wrong... but I think I have it sorted.

The aliens were tapping the side of their heads; I think that was their brains so they kept on tapping it. It could only be something to do with the brain but they gave signals to say that whatever was there left the heads and went into the clouds. They could only be on about either the mind, soul or spirit. They were also tapping on their foreheads – I think that was the mind," Savarnee said.

"Well, the mind is unlikely to leave the body. It was probably the soul or spirit," Adam said. "The spirit won't be here; it remains where it was at death on Earth," Adam went on with his lecture. We were ok as none of us really knew what happened when we died or were born so Adam continued.

"You have your mind when you're born and it stays with you and exists until you die. The soul, however, leaves your body when you die and might be able to be captured as a living entity that goes into a room and waits to be sorted and selected for another body to be born into."

"That's really interesting," Amanda said. "That must be it – the souls of dead people come here and are in a box. Well, not a box; maybe they're in the silver clouds of Sparkle. They are in boxes of a kind. You said they travelled around – maybe that was a safer place for them there. Just in there, waiting to be sorted and selected for bodies. I would think the mind will stay in the body."

Was it the souls, possibly in the clouds, that they were after? Nothing else existed on the planet. It could only be the souls they were after, but why? We had little knowledge about the soul; we knew it left the body when you died but where it went and what happened to it were starting to unfold.

Could our souls leave us and end off at Sparkle? Was Sparkle some kind of recycling planet for souls or was it deemed as heaven? Could we live our second lives in a silver cloud breezing around the atmosphere of Sparkle? Surely it was heaven's sorting house, built to process souls and designate them to the next newborn child at birth, completing the cycle into the human being for the next generation. This would all be happening in another dimension, out of the realms of our knowledge… it would have probably been like this from the start of time. The knowledge we had now was starting to open doors we previously didn't know existed. Were the silver clouds like a Tardis inside? Was there something beautiful happening inside them that was comfort to the souls in there?

We had all decided that, with Savarnee's testament regarding the communications with the aliens on Sparkle, we could now assume it was the souls of the deceased that were alive in the silver clouds of Sparkle. But what was the motive for the attacks against Sparkle? Was it to destroy the souls of the people past? They had indicated that the souls were souls from all species that had evolved, so was it a sorting room for the souls to be dispatched back down to Earth or to other planets and then be recycled into babies born, whether human or other? The riddle may just be becoming clearer…

We had all decided that the soul was an entity and it was a reusable item, like any other. The creator had made the souls for the people to be re-used for the benefit of the recipient. The knowledge of the precise being, whether human or other, would be wiped away and the new species would be granted life through the soul. With all this defined, our thoughts were on why the spaceships from Sphere were attacking Sparkle at the cost of losing alien beings and spaceships. Savarnee said there must be more than this. There had to be a reason why they wanted entry to Sparkle. Was it the fact they were locusts, going from planet to planet, taking the minerals and alien species and leaving the planet barren and lifeless like Intro, just leaving them as a base for their own use?

None of us could understand the logic in what was happening. It seemed a million miles away from common sense but I'm sure their intentions were not honourable. We had to go back to Sphere and see what species were targeting Sparkle and what their intentions were for the future. It was Blaise and Adam's turn to go, so they would have to go back to Sphere to see what was happening. Then, maybe, we could communicate with someone there and reach some kind of deal with them to stop the attacks against Sparkle. This was going to be a covert operation to find out who the first aliens on the planet were.

They would have to look for somewhere other than the assembly spaceship warehouses, and look more for where the aliens lived and worked, and where the current finished spaceships were. We could probably find out where the alien spaceships' commanders were and transform ourselves to look like them so we could talk and find out why they were desperate to get on to Sparkle. What resources did it hold and why were they so determined to get them?

Adam and Blaise were geared up and ready to go, Amanda said they had a dangerous assignment to do as it looked a secret guarded place where they were assembling spaceships. We knew now they were building battleships and out for war not space travel.

These were state of the art spaceships. They looked like troop carriers with the long slender middle, perfect for a few hundred troops to be in. They were armed so we had no reason to believe they were not carrying an attack force on board for when they got onto the surface of Sparkle.

Chapter 46

————◆————

Those gentle aliens would be slaughtered by the troops in the spaceships from Sphere. We needed to identify what the species looked like so we knew who these war-makers were. It seemed there would be no peace on Sparkle until these aliens had been destroyed forever. They were not good neighbours, Adam called in – they were at the back of Mars and about to enter Unimars, the gateway. It would not be too long before they reached Sphere. It was his last message before entering Unimars as we were maintaining silence from then on. It was a covert operation and we did not need to send messages that could be intercepted or triangulated to find our positions. The last thing we needed was to be caught.

We were on a roll and cruising past Intro. We could see Sphere in the distance. We were excited to be here but apprehensive as to what the outcome would be.

Our advantage was that we were virtually invisible and that was a big help to us to be able to move around the planet without being noticed. We had arrived at the entry point where we went in the last time. We were here, but the assembly plant was not the place we needed to be. We would have to scout the planet; it was all mostly industrial. They probably made some of the components here for the spaceships. We had not realised just how many factories there were here. We could see lots of what looked like nuclear power stations. They obviously needed power generation to build the components for the assembly of the spaceships.

We could see no other spaceships, just the same as before; like new cars in a car park ready to go to the dealer garage. We had to get closer to the area where the launch pads would be, although they were possibly able to take off from where they were parked up. We could only suck it and see. We had to return with the answers the group needed. We were rounding the other side of Sphere and there it was… it was a military base with barriers around it. Inside, there were houses that were really large. We had to go down and have a look. As we got closer, we could see they had sectioned areas off for a reason. We were not sure so we went for a closer look.

There was a large building not overlooked so we perched on the top of it. The building was some sort of storage place, so we went in through some vents in the roof. There was artificial atmosphere in the building – why would they create this here? The air on Sphere was not sufficient to sustain human life but we sensed the air in this unit was. We had trouble at internal roof level; there was something trapped under the roof. We had a few gaps there to get through and we managed to come below the obstruction and looked up to see what it was. To our amazement, we saw a silver cloud suspended there – had this come from Sparkle? We were not sure… it looked the same, but how could they have got it here to Sphere? Had they penetrated Sparkle at some time and taken the silver clouds? Did they have the same type of accommodation for souls on this planet?

We couldn't understand why it would be in this building when they were on Sparkle, a land that was beautiful and free. Here, it was contained in an artificial atmosphere in a horrible, grey-painted building. We assumed they would have different ways of holding their souls but this seemed to be the way planets in Unimars looked after the souls of their people. It made us wonder where our souls ended up in our galaxy. Could it be on Mars or Jupiter? Even Venus could be holding our souls ready for repatriation into newborns on Earth. Who was policing Sparkle and who had provided the satellites and the war machine? It had to have come from somewhere.

The aliens on Sparkle didn't look like they had done a good day's work there since they were born, although Sparkle was so immaculate. They couldn't have been untidy aliens; how they lived and what food they consumed was beyond our knowledge, and what was this silver cloud doing here on Sphere? Was it here to keep their souls in? It didn't look full like Sparkles, although we were not sure as to the population here; maybe it was a lot less than Sparkle.

We had no way to find out how to enter the silver cloud. Maybe there was a secret door, like in Sparkle's glitter ring. We needed to see what alien species were here, why they had created such an industrial planet and how they could exist here without a proper atmosphere.

We left the building the way we had come in, but we were in a quandary as to where to go. It was virtually ground coverage; there was not much open space here to see anything. We decided to move on a bit and see what more we could find. We rounded the side of Sphere and we could see a lot of activity. There seemed to be landing pads and spaceships on top of them, perched there ready to go. This was the space station; we would hopefully see alien species here now.

It was less dense in construction. There was a lot of open space where they could land and take off. There must have been twenty-five launch pads with spacecraft there on them. There were a few ready and we thought it would be a good idea to wait around and see what happened. Maybe there would be some maintenance staff fuelling or repairing or servicing the spaceships where they were, so we could hopefully catch someone coming to the craft. We were an hour into our wait and, sure enough, a spaceship came down to land.

"Got it," Adam said. "We have them now; they don't fly themselves."

We watched as the door opened on the side. We had just been lucky enough to pick the side with the exit.

Blaise said "Look! Look at them – they're flaming robots! They look like something else… look how they're walking. They look like us but are made completely out of metal. They're almost human."

"That's it," Adam said. "What is it that a robot can't do?"

Blaise said, "Think for themselves."

"That's it, that's what the silver cloud is here for. They want to steal the souls out of the silver clouds of Sparkle and keep them in their own silver cloud. It must have something in it that contains them like a prison and waits for a recipient but only deletes the memory of the last person when a recipient is found."

Chapter 47

————— ◆ —————

We now had what we thought was the answer – they wanted the souls in the robots. The aliens behind it were clever – their plan was probably to gain access to the souls in Sparkle's silver cloud; that's why they were so desperate to get through the defences. A robot that could think for itself would be a formidable enemy. It would be able to think outside the box it was in and the sky would be the limit. There would be no end to the places they could go or the things they could do. There would be no stopping them; they would be unbeatable. This was why they were losing so many spaceships; they were programmed to steer the spaceships but they would not be able to think how to take evasive action against the laser rays or any other weapon fired at them. With a soul and everything it had experienced, it would be a valuable asset for their robots, with a soul connecting all their movements and strategies to evade Sparkle's satellite defences and the power of the war machine.

It had all been thought out well. All they had to do was steal the souls from Sparkle. They wouldn't be happy on Sparkle when their souls had disappeared to Sphere and been imprisoned in a large warehouse, but at the moment, Sparkle was reasonably secure. The robots piloting the spacecraft could not fear or see danger. All they could do was what was programmed into them. They could not think at all.

As Blaise said to Adam, "If you can't think your way out of a situation, you can't get out of it."

They could have alien masters of the robots that might be able to outthink the defence systems in place. They had instructed the robots to attack Sparkle so they were more than half the way there, but attacking and gaining access through the defences of Sparkle was another nightmare for the robots of Sphere.

Now that we knew what they were up to, we probably knew more than the aliens on Sparkle about what was happening and why they were being invaded relentlessly. Maybe if they knew, they could send in the Doomsday Machine to take out all the production of spaceships on Sphere. If they had none left, it would all stop. However, they were not informed. If only we could tell them on Sparkle… would they even understand? We were trying to help them keep the souls of their deceased people.

Blaise was talking about how they got the souls into a silver cloud. There had to be a door... And how did the aliens controlling the robots on Sphere manage to even make one the same, ready for use, from the stolen souls from Sparkle? They must have had an idea of how successful they could be. Was it a matter of attacking Sparkle over and over until its defences had depleted? There was a strategy in place but only the aliens of Sphere knew it. I was sure it would be war again soon with Sparkle.

Someone would have known the amount of spacecraft Sphere had waiting to invade Sparkle. Adam had expressed interest in warning Sparkle about the silver cloud they had and their intentions of raiding their clouds for the souls of Sparkle's deceased. It would be sacrilege to see those souls ending up in the robots as they were out for war; it would not be a good place after the tranquil life they had lived on Sparkle. To end up in a dirty grey warehouse, trapped in a silver cloud with no escape, would not be an ideal place to be in your second life.

They must have been able to see the beauty of Sparkle as they floated around in the clouds. They were protected there in a bubble of tranquillity, which would all be gone if the robots managed to break the defences down. It would mean all the souls would then be gone; a soul could not live the same in a robot.

I thought they were not going to erase the information the souls had collected during a lifetime on Sparkle, but was not quite sure what would have been in the souls of the aliens on Sparkle. We were not sure if they had any experiences at all for the souls to grow knowledge.

Looking over at the aliens' launch pads, we decided to risk it and get a bit closer to the spaceships to see if there was anybody inside them. We parked on a storage area where there were some black bags; they must have used them for carrying weapons, rockets or laser cartridges for backup power for the spaceship's lasers. There were lots of them stacked up around the site. There was some writing on the bags so we were inquisitive enough to take a look. As we got closer, we could see it was written in English and said 'Detroit Funeral Services'. There was another – 'Detroit Hospital Morgue'. There was one labelled 'New York Sleep Easy Funeral Services'.

We started to look at them all. We could see these could not have got there on their own. It looked like they must have visited Earth to get the souls of the dead people. They must have replaced them with other dead people they had brought there the night before the soul left their bodies, transported them to Sphere, harvested their souls and returned them to the mortician before they were cremated. A new cycle of souls were then taken again, so possibly there were souls already in the silver cloud here in the warehouse. They were probably after Sparkle as it was full and could provide souls for as many robots as they needed without going backwards and forwards to Earth to steal them and risk being caught.

It would be easier to target Sparkle and take the souls in the clouds there.

Adam said, "I wondered where our souls go when we die".

In unison, we both thought, 'Here in Unimars... Sparkle... that's where they go and someone is defending them from robot attacks'. The clouds were full of souls from Earth; that's why they wanted them. Their souls had matured over the years and that, to a robot, is liquid gold. They would be able to keep the knowledge and transfer the soul into the robots; then, there would be no stopping them. They would be victorious in war everywhere they wanted to go.

They would use the souls and their knowledge to put into robots. The souls, believing they were still part of the old hosts, would be directing the robots' strategies or learning new ones. The robots would eventually be able to conquer all species on all the planets. What soldiers they would have! They didn't need to eat or drink – just a bit of maintenance. They could wage war wherever they could as they didn't need air to breathe – the perfect killing machine.

They obviously needed the souls for the robot soldiers or pilots of the spaceships. There would be people on Earth from all walks of life.

Blaise said, "Yes, but what are we missing here? If this is some satellite holding place for souls from Earth, if they use these souls in the robots, how are we going to recycle the souls for our new generation on Earth?"

There would be none to recycle – they would all be in the robots, which would not be wiping clean the slate in the souls but using the information to expand their foothold for galaxy control. It was robots flying the humanoids into Intro for food for the spiders, but were the spiders native to Intro or was it the humanoids that were the native species? Had they been kidnapped from the opposite side of Intro and ferried around to where the spiders were? Were they being cultivated by the robots in some macabre way to breed them like cattle for food? If they could do this to them, they could do it to people on Earth. We could be the food for the next generation of spiders.

Chapter 48

———◆———

Blaise said, "If we have no souls, then as a race, we will die as there would be no souls to recycle."

We could not exist without them and it's what keeps our lives together and defines who we are. Without a soul, we would have no identity, personality or memories. We could survive but it would be a practical death. We would have no emotions, consciousness or normality in our lives. The new humans born without a soul could live no differently than the aliens on Sparkle. It was a halfway house for storage of souls for new humans, not for robots.

They were never part of the maker's remit; they were a workforce made for work and war – never to be human in their thinking. We could not tolerate this. We would be extinct as a race in 100 years if the robots took our souls. They would leave us with nowhere to go or think. We would be worse than the aliens on Sparkle, just there to live, not evolving beyond what they probably had always been. The creator had decided to use this planet as a place of storage to keep the journey short to save the souls until they got to Sparkle.

We needed to get back to Earth and out of Sphere in case we were spotted. We could not afford to lose the information we had. Unbelievably, they had been visiting our places of the dead and stealing them for their souls then returning the soulless corpses. Without souls, we were not going to be able to look after ourselves and it would threaten the future of the entire human race.

We would have no normality or knowledge of how to live. We would have no capacity to remember actions we had just done… we wouldn't remember how to do anything but exist for a short time. We would probably never reach adulthood. We would be virtual cabbages, knowing nothing, remembering nothing, and with no identity and no personality. How could we exist as a species? Animals would be more adapted to life than us. We would be virtually cavemen on a planet that could not sustain life, even for a few years, without agriculture to grow food and feed the world.

We had to go back to the team and tell them our unbelievable story. We left Sphere and made our way back to Earth, Adam and I talking out the horrors of what we had found, that it would make the robots strong and the earthlings weak and primitive like the humanoids, food for whatever the robots wanted to feed – creatures like the spiders. We would not be able to fight them if we saw them coming. Within seconds, our memory of them would be gone. We would be lucky to have the memory of a goldfish, lasting only a few seconds. This would be a planet of food resources for the spiders or others. It would be our fault if we didn't halt the spaceship production.

We could not let the spaceships invade Sparkle any more. It was now in our interests to make sure the robots, and their masters, could not advance towards Earth or colonise any other planets. We had to stop them in their tracks. They could not be allowed to destroy Sparkle's defences. We could try and help Sparkle eliminate the robots from Sphere, and all their production lines. We could destroy all the spaceships and the assembly plants and that would buy Earth more time. We were no longer just out there flying a kite – we were now hopefully going to save Earth as we know it, but how were we going to tell the authorities on Earth? That was a bigger problem than the robots themselves.

We would have to discuss this later as right now, we had rounded Mars and could see a safe route all the way back to Earth. As we passed Mars, there was molten liquid spewing out of the hole the laser made. This was not the sign of a dead planet but an evolving one. The planet was too young and hot to accept new life so our take on our planets here in our solar system, the Milky Way, was that we were younger than Unimars. The planets we had visited showed no sign of volcanic activity so they must have cooled and consolidated to rock. They could have been 10's millions of years older than our galaxy. Nobody apart from the team would ever believe us.

We had put it all together and the future looked grim for Earth as a planet. We had also discovered that the Milky Way was only a young galaxy and not the oldest. It had around 10 million more years to mature and cool down itself before it would sustain life. Unimars was probably the Milky Way's great-great-grandfather as galaxies go. All the planets here were looking like they were habitable in some form without the need to build cities underground or needing to deal with toxic atmospheres.

We had to decide between us all what we could do now. We could not tell the authorities – they would lock us up and throw away the key and we would never be coming out of prison again. However, if we didn't act, the world as we know it would die. The human race would be extinct in a short time; everyone on Earth would be no more than an empty vessel walking around with no direction or purpose. They would all be more or less zombies living purely on what they could salvage to keep them alive. It would be down to us to try and defend Sparkle and save our supply of souls contained in the silver clouds. How we were going to do it remained a mystery at the moment. We could not make war on another planet in another galaxy; there would only be five people who would know we were at war but the consequences would be dire for us and Earth.

If we caused a war with Sphere, we had no idea what force they had to be reckoned with but we could not let them destroy Earth by taking the souls of our departed to put in robots to make them able to think for themselves like humans. That would make them really dangerous and they would conquer Earth fast if they had the capacity of a human being. We had come from the maker and he had given us the will to think and be able to do amazing things to keep us alive and give us a long life to live.

There was probably no comparison in the galaxies... we were unique in what we could do and invent. It would be a team discussion as to where to take this situation we found ourselves in. If the robots of Sphere and their masters got hold of the souls on Sparkle, they might not be able to keep them alive as their silver cloud may not sustain the souls like Sparkle could. They had been the caretakers for our souls as a satellite place to reserve for Planet Earth. There could be no walking away now, but we had no mandate to go to war with Sphere or any other planet.

We were not peacekeepers of the galaxy but we could see the writing on the wall and it wasn't reading well. We had to do something, but who would believe anything we did or said? They would never believe that they could be extinct in 100 years or before if they couldn't live and feed themselves. We could be a species of cannibals, eating each other, living on a barren planet with no agriculture to grow food, no clean water to drink, no medicines. We wouldn't be able to remember to take them even if we had them! We would go back millions of years yet never have the souls even cavemen had. It was a total mess but only we had the knowledge and tools to sort it out. The rest of Earth was still trying to get back to the moon and Mars. They had not moved on in the leaps and bounds we were at now. We all had to meet and discuss our way forward. We were in a dilemma as to what to do; there was no impending war, but what the robots could do would finish off the Earth as we know it.

Chapter 49

The species and robots from Sphere would only have to wait a few years until we had no more souls and they would just walk onto Earth with no retaliation from the humans. They would not be capable of putting a strategy together to defeat the invading force. There would be no point in an attack whilst the armies on Earth were strong; they would probably wait until they were at their weakest and come in then. We were facing oblivion in the wake of an invading species; Earth would soon belong to Sphere and the human race could be used as a food source to feed spiders to help with the spaceship program Sphere was promoting.

We were on our way back to Earth and, on the main run in, Mars was still spewing out molten lava as we passed. However, it seemed to be slowing down in its trail over the surface. It was consolidating as it cooled. The Milky Way was definitely evolving as a galaxy, But the thought crossed our minds was this the beginning of the end? We had wondered for a long time if space travel was a possibility. Would the day come when we could explore the neighbouring galaxies, or was space just to remain a star-gazer's paradise, full of wonder and magical beauty?

Well, it had come... As long as it was in the remit of how far the brain could project us and keep us connected to the body, that would now have to be put on the back burner. We had other problems to sort out – saving the Earth from certain destruction from Sphere.

We had arrived back in the laboratory. Adam and I had been communicating all the way back from Mars and we had so many thoughts to relay back to the team; however, none of it was good news. Everything we had to tell them affected everybody on Earth, never mind the team. What we had discovered was immensely important. Things were already at a critical stage and we were in fear for Earth's domination if Sparkle was to be defeated and the knowledge of the souls in the robots was increased. They would be unstoppable; undefeatable by any species. They wanted to take over the universe and enslave everyone that lived on the planets they visited. We needed an emergency meeting the moment we arrived; it was time-sensitive as nothing was going to wait.

Attacks by the spaceships were now a daily thing and how long could the Doomsday Machine keep them at bay? They seemed relentless in their attacks and would eventually find a way to destroy the last defences of Sparkle. Once the Doomsday Machine was destroyed, they would easily overtake the satellite defences and invade Sparkle. There would be nothing stopping them after that. The production line would have to be stopped on Sphere to prevent them reaching their goal of obtaining all the souls stored there in the silver clouds.

As soon as we arrived, the team were already asking questions. We decided to stay late to discuss all our thoughts and findings. Everyone was so concerned about what we had put together, so we had to be careful or it could lead us to make rash decisions. We could not afford to make those; we would really have to think it through. Going to war with Sphere was not an option. Apart from the laser weapon we had, they had easier access to Earth with their spaceships and could virtually obliterate the human race. We didn't want them on our doorstep. We hadn't any defences in space to be able to protect us and a nuclear-powered weapon would not be a good defence against Sphere's spaceships.

They were well geared up for war; they could just pick us off from space with their lasers. Once we used our laser against them, they would have the location of our laser and target that location and destroy us *and* the laser. If we were going to war with Sphere, we could hide in Unimars and give the co-ordinates of the spaceships and let the laser tracker take them out. They might be able to find out it came from Earth but would not be able to track its location, and, providing we could be hidden from them, they would not be able to defend themselves against it.

We had arrived at a conclusion that the only way forward to save Earth was to use the laser to destroy their production of the spaceships. If we did this, they would have no way of attacking Sparkle or Earth. They would not have the capability of attack and, if we could stop future production, we could rest peacefully that our souls were safe on Sparkle. There must have been a reason why they travelled so far to store the souls, so it would all be in the lap of the gods as to how we would come out of a war with Sphere. To be defeated would not be an option. If they won, they would take our planet straight away. There would be no mercy for anybody left on Earth.

We had to destroy their capability of going anywhere else and colonising other planets. It was all possible through the laser. We would only be observers giving out the co-ordinates for the laser to track the target. It was easier on Sphere as, unlike Sparkle, it had no defences, so if we gave the co-ordinates, we could hit the target precisely. Would we be saving Sparkle or would it one day fall to other invading species? Was defending Sparkle going to become a regular occurrence, and did they really need our help or could the Doomsday Machine deal with the attacking forces? It seemed to destroy everything it fired at – was it more than just the monster spaceship it looked like? Did it contain more technology than we realised?

Some superior force was at work somewhere to produce such a spaceship; this was the mother of them all. It was just a killing machine, there to bring death and destruction to whatever got in its way. Did we, as a species alien to Unimars, need to be involved in this war between the two planets? Couldn't we just sit on the sidelines waiting for Sphere to take over Sparkle? It would be risky to get through the defences on Sparkle. It was not clearly accessible due to the glitter rings surrounding it, and we could not go to any authorities on Earth for permission to laser an alien species, even if the majority were robots with no feelings. It was decided between us that no nation had a 'need to know' and things would be treated on a need-to-know basis.

We were going to take it in turns to find out the best location for being able to see Sphere and co-ordinate the laser ray as it was fired. It would be just short bursts of rays travelling through space to Sphere, a deadly course, but not really traceable. We had seen their power on Mars and the depth it penetrated into the surface of the planet. If we could increase the spread of the ray before it hit its target, it would be more effective in destroying more industrial areas and buildings. We could take out other areas as the planet came around full circle. It appeared they turned like Earth, as they were always slightly changed when we arrived at slightly different times.

They probably had the same time orbit around the sun in Unimars. It was yet to be monitored as we were concentrating on more important things at this time. We were more concerned about saving Earth than worrying about whether the planets moved the same as Earth in a twenty-four-hour cycle and an annual cycle. We could only guess at this time, but as long as they were turning sufficiently for us to hit targets on them, we were happy. We did not think we could track the laser around the rear of Sphere, although we had not tried. It might lose the power emitted if curving too much; a straight line would always be the best way to guarantee results.

We would be testing out the ray behind the port side of Mars to see if it would hit a target opposite to the first hit we had made on the surface. This shot would go around to the side of it. It would be Amanda and Anthony who were going this time. Blaise would be on the laser with Adam and Savarnee, whilst Amanda and Anthony would pick out a series of locations to see if the laser was effective in all areas, not just Mars. We would look for a star that was close and use it as a target as there were millions of them in the sky. With the gases they emitted, they lit up the sky in a display of wonderful splendour of twinkling lights as far as the eye could see. The further we travelled, the more stars we could see. Space was full of them – millions of them.

We had so much to discover in our galaxy, never mind the universe. Space was endless – no top, no bottom or sides. It was just a vast place with no end to its boundary. If we did pass our galaxy, would we find another universe? Behind everything we discovered in ours, there could be thousands of universes and hundreds of thousands of galaxies in them. We were now in a place where it was only the brave, not the faint-hearted that would survive here. It was the fear of the unknown that would be the demise of others who could not do and go where we were going.

Chapter 50

—————◆—————

We were pioneers of space; everybody knew the risks they were taking and the risks had now increased dramatically into espionage and a mission to save Earth from Sphere and their intentions to steal our souls. We were now on full alert to get ready to destroy the capability of Sphere to attack other planets. We had become the guardians of space; we were about to declare war on Sphere and we were tooling up for that war. We tested five locations and every one was a perfect hit. We had the laser on maximum power but we could not afford to have Mars on fire, bringing too much attention to the planet from other alien species. After all, even on our first attempt at space travel, we had seen spaceships travelling through our galaxy.

That time had gone and we had moved on now and we were miles ahead of ourselves. We had concluded that the ray was really good and Blaise had done an exceptional job of creating it. The ray was deadly – if it hit its target everywhere, there would be no way of getting away from it, especially when it was coming at you at twice the speed of light. One thing worried us – was it too powerful to fight a war with? It would probably destroy the whole planet or cause it to break up if it was hit too many times.

We would have to make sure we picked our targets carefully; a prolonged attack would weaken Sphere and it could break up and crash into Sparkle and all would have been to no avail. We had to ensure that casualties were kept to a minimum. We could not be wiping out species; they could be the only kind of aliens on Sphere, as we had not encountered the robot masters yet.

We would have to keep the secret forever. We would have to disappear into space if we were ever found out. The authorities would never let us off and say we had done the right thing. There would never be the right time to go to war with another race of aliens.

We were going to give it a week: Meanwhile, we would just do some reconnaissance work on Sphere and then attack them next week. We would have to map out how we were going to track the laser at different times to make sure we had our co-ordinates set for a specific time, then Blaise could fire the laser at the co-ordinates set, and we would be near to ensure the target was destroyed. We were going to take out all the factories and the spaceships on the landing pads, along with the warehouse holding the silver cloud in it. If they lost that one, they would have nothing to put the souls into.

We spent a week mapping and sorting exact co-ordinates for the right time so the target was right where we were going to laser. Monday morning would be World War Three. We had to save the souls from attack from Sphere and we were ready to fight. We would show no mercy and take no prisoners; everyone would be obliterated. They were so close to getting access to Sparkle and the souls in the silver clouds That we just couldn't let it go. We could not let the Earth humans die as a race; we were only defending ourselves from extinction.

The spaceships were first on our list. If they were destroyed first, they would not have any craft to find us, so that would be our first target. We messaged Blaise to fire on the coordinates given. Before we had even finished the message, we saw a blinding flash of light hit the area where the spaceships were. He had hit the mark. The spaceships were on fire, exploding all over. We could sense the explosions. As the bursts of laser fire came and destroyed all of the craft, we were sending more co-ordinates to Blaise and he was taking them all out.

The mission was accomplished here; all the spaceships had been obliterated. We moved on fast to the warehouse where the silver cloud was, and again, in a split second, it was destroyed. The laser was lethal, taking out wide swathes of factory units. The spaceships on the assembly line were being destroyed; there was nothing left. We could sense the bursts of the laser hitting their targets; there was carnage everywhere.

Nothing would be flying from here again for a hundred years. We were going to send the co-ordinates for the cities so that we could take them out as well. Blaise was there again, as deadly as a spitting cobra. Everything was on fire in a rage of destruction. They had never witnessed a total annihilation like this before. The cities were being taken out as well as all the landing craft, spaceships and the silver cloud; it was all gone. The planet was on fire and burning out of control.

What had we done? We had saved Earth for a number of years but what if they could put it back together fast and be in production again? We had seen the way the robots built the spaceships; they were like a car assembly line. They would have to be on our checklist to keep monitoring them to ensure they would no longer be a danger to us again.

We had given Earth a chance to advance to be ready for an attack if it came in the future. The aliens would be trying to check where the laser had come from. They would never believe that it could have come from Earth as they visited to steal our souls from the deceased. They would be looking at our forms of transport and thinking we were still fairly primitive in our ways and still using electricity and fossil fuels to generate the power we have. They would never believe the capability we have now. We would now have to look out for aliens in our hospitals and morgues looking for the souls of our dead people. How could we explain to authorities that we knew aliens were taking our souls? We did not know, but we would have to find a way of stopping them.

Blaise copied in: "I know they try to get here on a regular basis so I will laser the spaceships on their way in. I will at least stop them from using the souls in some robots somewhere."

We would have to try and protect our souls on Sparkle. The inhabitants of Sparkle would be so happy the planet Sphere had been cleared of the attacking forces. On Sparkle, everything now would be good for us. We could use it as a base to explore new planets in Unimars and we could at least relax for the short term. Now, we were going to start heading back to Earth and we could relax as all the spacecraft from Sphere had been reduced to dust on the planet.

We were on a roll! As we came out, we turned to port as we left Sphere. All was good moving towards Intro, when suddenly, three spaceships were on our starboard side and they made moves to come down to us. They had probably picked us up by our signals and now they were after us. They were firing their lasers at us and they were getting very close to us, despite how small we were. We were in trouble. We had to be able to get away from them but they were keeping up with us. The spacecraft looked different; a lot sleeker and smaller; more of an attack space-ship. These were built for war. They must have had every weapon going on them; they looked menacing and they were after us.

They had obviously picked up our signals to base and now we were being attacked and they were close enough to touch. We had to try and manoeuvre out the way before they could fire. We had to get them off our tails so we could speed up but they were at the side of us, under us like an escort. We were trapped! There was only one way out and we went for it – a vertical climb between them all. We let go and shot up into space at vertical lightning speed; we were so lucky they did not have the power to follow us.

We managed to get clear of them and made a diversion to take them off our trail so as not to lead them back to Earth… but they were out there looking for us. We could sense their presence as we back-tracked. They were still looking but we were aware that to be obscure is a good thing. We were clear and would live to fight another day. Our concern was, where did these war spacecraft come from? Were they just late back to Sphere or were they from another planet in another galaxy? Was there a connection with Sphere? Had they been sent to deal with us?

Milton Keynes UK
Ingram Content Group UK Ltd.
UKHW031117251024
450128UK00003B/56